I0685612

ANGEL SHOT

A RIPPTON U DARK ROMANCE

RIPPTON CREATIVES

SOFIA AVES

First Edition

Cover Art by JayJay Book Designs

EBOOK ISBN 978-1-923471-82-5

PRINT ISBN 978-1-923471-24-5

CONTENT WARNING

Key and Kash are some of Rippton U's most notorious fixtures. In almost every book, they are hated, and shunned. Most characters run when they see them and to make deals with these devils is to court death in a literal sense. But these albino twins also served their own book and their own twisted sort of Happily Ever After. That does, however, come with its own sort of warning system.

Please be aware that in reading Angel Shot you may encounter:

Menage scenes and Poly relationships
    Serial Killers
    Non c*n

Knife violence

Death

Forced orgasms

Anal Play

Inflatable toys

Recounting of sexual abuse

Murder

Gun violence

Exhibitionism

Voyerisom

Double Penetration

MM kink play

Humiliation and degradation

Goddess worship

Boot licking

Soaking and cock warming

Somnophilia

Stalking

Twisted hero complex

If you feel dark romance is a fun place to read, please turn out the lights. This not a place for shades of grays, or morally skewed characters. Key and Kash are all fucked up, and they know it.

Enjoy.

Sofia xx

BLURB

She's the light to our shadow. The addiction we crave.
Our toy, even if she doesn't know that yet.
Helia Mascot is the perfect girl.
No friends, except one. No family who cares. No life.
Forgotten. Alone.
She exists in her art, tortured by darkness when
everyone else sleeps.
But we won't let her be forgotten any longer.
And we won't let her be alone.
Helia is part of our game, one of our deals.
And once she's made a deal with us, it's a promise
that can't be unmade.
We will come to collect, and when we do, she'll be
ours, even if that's not what she wants...
At first.

Escape is a pretty cage. Ours is forever.
We've never wanted anyone like we want her. It'll be
so much fun to watch her try to run.

To the nightmares we miss before we wake

PROLOGUE

KEY

"I have a car. You can have it. I won't report it stolen, I promise. *I promise.*"

Every word is a little more panicked, a little more desperate.

A little more delicious.

Life drips from the man seated before me because he looked at her. Last week, he dared to *touch her*. Not that he has a clue what he's done wrong, or why he'll die. Neither does she, but we'll get around to that. Later. Right now it's fun to watch him beg. It amuses me to pretend to consider his plea. That spark of hope, like what he says might actually matter.

The bargains he strikes in his last moments,

when true despair lingers in the air like the bitterest acid. His final flavor.

"Mmm." I tap my blade to my lips and lick the tip. His blood is sour. I won't make that mistake again. Tainted, because he touched her. No, the faster I kill this sack of depleted air and move along to more fascinating prey, the better. "I have..."

Other things to do today.

If I tell him what's on the agenda for today, his spark of hope will die.

Just like him.

I smile around my blade, then fold and pocket it. Breath leaves my toy's lungs as though I've done him a favor. Not that I have, really, swapping the slim metal for something more...brutal. The brass knuckles that fit my hand, custom made, of course. The irregular cuts in the metal will stamp my name across his flesh. Once, maybe, before his face becomes pulp.

A fitting epitaph for the man with no name. That's how he will remain. Unfound and unnamed. How he will be reported. Because, even with this piece of shit's pathetic offer, I have more money than I know what to do with. Usually. The deals I make with my twin are for fun. My version, of course, not some vanilla business deal like Beau Bennet's as he plays with his Kingsmen.

No, I'll pay for my piss-stained man-toy to stay nameless. Family-less.

Found by no one.

A smile threatens my face, but I hold the peaceful expression back. He can see my joy later, when I ruin his precious perfect frat boy, paid for, too-white teeth before he bleeds out on the warehouse floor.

A rental that connects me to nothing and no one, paid for in cash by the hour. Like a whore, only for me the money flows in the other direction, and my time is worth more.

And his is almost up.

I crouch before him, my face serious. "What can you offer me?" *Nothing.*

His eyes gleam, fanatical. Frantic. "Everything."

You touched what I desire most.

"What you own?" My softest, considering tone.

You are nothing. Pathetic, piss boy.

"Take it all."

Because daddy will give you more. I killed mine, left him gurgling in a puddle of his own drool and fluids for touching someone else who belongs to me.

"So...sweet."

His labored breath hitches as he catches on. This isn't going his way. And now, he knows.

I will end you.

Sometimes, I like to get hands on. Sometimes, I like to get messy.

Tonight is one of those nights.

"Helia is mine." *Even if she doesn't know that yet.*

"Who?" His eyes widen, playing the innocent. Only he was never innocent, even if she is.

Wrong answer, frat fucker.

My metal enhanced fist finds soft flesh, splitting the soft layer to the bone. Coating my hand in his precious, rich boy blood. Old blood.

So, so worthy.

You will be nameless. Forgotten. Because you touched her before me.

Flesh softens, tenderized beneath my cold rage. Metal to bone, skin to skin.

It's a messy night.

Soon, he makes no sound at all. And our hour is up.

CHAPTER ONE

HELIA

The art stool beside me sat conspicuously empty. Conspicuous, because Ethan never missed a class. Empty, because...well.

Ethan *never* missed a class.

He'd been my mini stalker all semester at Rippton U—for most of my second year and well into my third, come to think of it. And now that he wasn't there, my table seemed vacant.

Too quiet.

Keeping my head down, I ignored the rest of my class and painted in black. Black on black. Gray on black. Mixed in white that became gray that merged into shadow.

The same shadows that I watched, the shadows

that waited beneath my windows last night as they did every night. I knew I wasn't imagining them, or maybe I was, in my sleepless, insomniac state. Hell, I even tried to paint one, after I hallucinated it—them —coming into my room, bending over my bed and pressing a soft kiss to my lips.

And woke with a soft cry on my tingling mouth that related to nothing in my vacant room.

Empty, empty, empty.

Just like my life.

My lips weren't the only thing that tingled, or were damp that night. I worked myself to a furious orgasm that ruined as fast as the elusive dream faded, frustrated with myself, and screamed into my pillow for all the wrong reasons. The same emotion slammed me again now as my brush jabbed at my blacks, stroked more onto the board.

I opted to use that over a canvas, preferring the smoother strokes. I knew that if I looked out of the window and peered around a bit, I'd see them, the twins. Key and Kash. The college's feral pair of disruptors at their best, and at worst... They liked to do their deals near this building nearest dusk. My classroom just happened to be the prime hunting ground for their favorite twisted pastime.

I shivered as the last of the light left campus in a

perpetual purple haze that would only last a few more minutes before the world darkened, just like my painting. Then the campus lights would flicker on in a false show of brightness, and Rippton's nightlife would begin. I hated the fakeness of it all, and wished for the first time that Ethan was here, to keep me company, no matter how much I usually despised him.

The rest of the class who chattered on, unfocused, and melted away as I painted on, until it was only me and my work, the shadow that emerged on the black landscape before me. Drawing me in, calling to me.

My breaths grew shorter as I started into the faceless hood that lingered, just out of sight. Beckoning, though no hand was raised. As if it, *the shadow*, who knew that I wanted to see the features beneath.

To know who watched me at night.

Probably, it was some drug dealer who loitered around my off campus building, well away from security. Who wanted to make their own sorts of deals.

I stayed away from those, too. Not because I liked the way my art flowed better when my mind was my own, but because I hated the lack of control over my own body under the influence of the drug, whatever the chosen poison of the moment might be.

My headspace fuzzed at the edges as I sank deeper into my mood with the impending night. Not the best time to make art, maybe. I'd always preferred morning classes when the light was better. The artificial glow bothered me with its incessant hum on so many levels. One of the perks of living alone and off campus, maybe. Or maybe I was simply the spoilt, abandoned daughter of rich parents who lived their lives independent of anything that resembled family values. Parents who preferred to dump their offspring into her own life years early.

Because unlike the rest of Rippton U, I wasn't the same age as the rest of the student body. About to complete my third year and I just turned eighteen. Under the select tutelage of many teachers and extra mentors, I flourished with my absentee parents and a distinct lack of friends groups through high school. And when the advance invitations to the country's most influential college arrived, I took it without thinking. Now, knowing what I did about Rippton U, maybe I should have asked questions instead of being a sixteen year old with stars in her eyes. And so my age remained a secret that I kept to myself, along with the rest of my solitary life.

Well, mostly solitary. An anchorite artist could choose to have a select hermit friend or two, right? Only the singular altar I worshiped at was that of my art and the shadows that watched me, if only in the darkest hours when sleep evaded me. When the constant state of exhaustion kicked in, along with an excess of caffeine.

"You paint alone today, Miss Mascot?" David Magnus, the art professor who prefers the term "Master" Magnus, the fucking freaker, leaned over my work. His loose shirt dangled close to my wet paint. Too close.

My hands hovered instinctively forward as I mantled over my work, protective like a hawk. "I don't have control over who attends your class," I managed, as soon as I was sure he hadn't damaged anything. I held back the urge to grab his shirt and tuck it in but that would be seen as...inappropriate and I didn't do contact with anyone, almost, despite my weekly Tuesday night attempt at dating which failed yet again this week.

How sad can my life possibly be?

Abandoned by parents, the stalker-obsessed art student who I couldn't stand, and now Taco Tuesday sucked as well. Just casket me up, baby. Actually, that gave me a fresh idea. I flipped open my folio, grabbed a charcoal from my set and sketched an outline. A few angles and some shadow and I had the start of something...

Something that was slightly obscene.

A teddy dangling from an open casket beneath a lamppost. I had no idea why the lamppost was there. It just appeared. The teddy felt right and that was what mattered at the end. Maybe he was comfy in the casket. Maybe he was warm, and homeless. What a ridiculous, absurd notion.

I fucking loved it.

"You are..." David Magnus trailed off. He caught the corner of my folio with one pristine fingertip that looked as though it had never seen ink, paint or charcoal. "What is this meant to be?"

I grimaced at the sketch, wishing I'd kept the fragment of imagination inside my head. Showing incomplete art before I'd thought out its purpose was always a mistake. *Always.*

"Ah, a teddy in a coffin?" I offered my professor, as I placed my charcoal back in my container, closing the lid gently. The tin scraped on itself, drawing eyes around the room.

My elbows pressed to my sides. I hated being the

centre of any kind of attention, and *Master* Magnus seemed to enjoy singling me out at every opportunity. Something that Ethan and I both hated. The attention was unwelcome for both of us, if for different reasons.

"A teddy. In a coffin," he repeated, drawing out the single syllables until I sank on my stool. "This is what three years of fine arts education amounts to in your eyes, Miss Mason?" His hand brushed across my freshly painted work, smearing the blacks into grays. My hooded figure—already faint, and hidden in the shadows—merged with the darkness, and disappeared.

Paint smeared the heel of his hand, but he pretended not to notice as though his action had been unintentionally accidental.

We both knew it wasn't.

You. Fucking. Asshole.

But I needed his class in order to graduate, and so I bit my lip, and said nothing. The ultimate roll over. Maybe my next art work should be belly white. That would suit the mood, at least.

"Better luck next time, Miss Mason," he murmured, as though I hadn't put four weeks of work into the painting he just ruined.

I stared up at him, knowing our interaction

didn't go unnoticed by the rest of the class that had fallen more silent than ever. The usual brushstrokes and soft rustles, almost musical in their regularity, ceased.

And I was the center of everyone's attention, yet again. Yay for me. At least, this time. I would earn that place.

"Thank you for screwing with my peace, Master Magnus," I murmured into the hush that thickened with every word I spoke. My courage came from somewhere, even if I didn't quite understand that place just yet. My heart hammered inside my chest cavity. *You need this class. Do not fuck it up.* But he'd fail me, regardless. I may as well walk right now. Ethan, of all people, might be my guiding force, but he wasn't here to prevent catastrophe tonight.

And so, as always, I went it alone.

"Be careful, Miss Mascot." David Magnus matched my soft tone, my calm outlook. Perhaps we were just two academics, discussing future events, rather than my specific fate.

Or maybe we weren't.

"If this is the path you continue along, my class may not be the best place for you to allow your... particular brand of creative freedom to flourish in." The corner of his mouth curled up in derision.

A sycophantic snicker that sounded like the color brown originated from the front of the studio.

I shook my head, letting my black hair fall back, knowing that paint caught in it, adhering some of the strands together. "If this is how you treat your students, disrespecting their art, then I'm not sure I wish to be a part of your class," I replied, maintaining the decorum of the status quo.

Somewhere outside the room yet still nearby, I swore I heard a low laugh.

If my professor wanted to be the first to break it and lose his temper, he could be my guest.

Master Magnus's face reddened. "Your time in my classroom has ended, Miss Mascot. Please take your work, for the little it is worth, and get. Out." He practically spat the last two words in a temper tantrum at me for not getting his way, seething as he lorded his height over me.

The hour ticked over, and the grandfather clock in the hall beyond that I'd always hated, but appreciated in this moment, began its eighteenth hour chime. "Timing," I murmured, as everyone gathered their things, casting curious glances my way. Perhaps measuring whether I would grovel my way back into Magnus's good graces, or bribe my way back in.

I could. All it would take was a phone call to

daddy. Hell, even a text message would do it. But I was done. I'd find another way to cover the hole in my third year plan.

"*Out*," Magnus hissed.

I rose, collected my bag and my charcoals, and looked down at my smudged painting. At the threat hidden in shadow that no one could see anymore. Somehow, I liked it better this way. "A gift," I said lightly, knowing what came next.

"I'll toss it the moment you leave the building," Master Magnus said, oh so freaking predictably.

I shrugged, and aimed my body toward the door, keeping my steps small. *Five, six, seven—*

"Or, perhaps I'll leave it behind a stack of boards where it will remain, dusty and unused for a decade, alongside the work of other mediocre students who have walked out of this room and disappeared into obscurity. Names forgotten, just like their withering talent." The spite that laced his voice froze everybody in the room, including me.

What a hateful little asshole you really are.

Perhaps it was Magnus I'd painted in the hood, but then, I'd never gift him such prime real estate. No, that sought after position belonged to someone else. Who, I had no idea, but certainly not him.

I rotated on my heel to face him as the soft kiss of

night air drifted through an open window accompanied by the faint scent of spice-tinged weed. "Please do. I'm sure it will sit nicely next to yours in that mass of obscurity collecting dust."

The insult tumbled too-freely from my poisonous lips. David Magnus's eyes flashed with the sort of hatred that I thought only happened in movies. Then my feet moved me across the floor and out the door with me an observer only in my own exodus.

And in the narcotics laced air, I swore the echo of the laugh I'd heard before followed me from the art studio.

CHAPTER TWO

KASH

Helia was a fucking goddess. I'd kneel to worship at her feet, but she trotted across campus too fast after her altercation with her lecturer. I walked away after the first part of her class, leaving my twin to listen in. He could stay and contemplate the future of the man who I refused to call *professor,* as if he was even worthy of the title given to his colleagues. I had another job tonight to occupy my time that took me away from sweet Helia. But I would return to her soon.

Mind, the girl that my twin and I followed around campus like a fucking pair of puppies attracted plenty of attention. The sort who wanted more than a little look while she sat in art class, painting prettily away. The sort who wasn't content to simply *see*.

The sort who needed to touch.

And that was never okay.

Her little art friend found out the hard way. He liked to touch, and he liked to do far more than look. Because he liked to *steal*.

It turned out that Art Buddy Ethan had an obsession to rival ours.

No. That was an outright lie. I should punish myself, but later. After I washed away the blood that coated every pore in my arms. I toed the body out of the way as I moved around, keeping my steps small, my feet on the plastic I'd laid out for this particular event.

Ethan hadn't made a whole lot of sound. He hadn't fought much, either. In fact, he only said one thing that I still mulled over, as though it baffled him:

"I thought it would be both of you."

Strange words, for a strange college student.

Usually, the Rippton cadre screamed and begged for their lives, or offered some ridiculous—and often, lowball—amount of payment in order to keep their pithy lives intact. That tactic never worked, of course. But on the rare occasion, someone offered something we didn't have, and we... kept them. Like a prized puppy.

And once. Just once, we let that person run free.

I still wasn't sure if that had been a mistake or an interesting turn in life. But right now I needed to clean up before Key berated me for my mess—again.

Helia Mascot had been a long running obsession of ours. Unhealthy, unusual and unseen. All the things that made us...

Well, us.

She was perfection in every way. Pretty, in an unintentional, gothic princess sort of way with the elfin, delicate features, and the eye of an artist who sees the world from a skewed perspective, rather than taking reality at face value like so many others. Eyes hollow from internal pain and torture, the kind that we often dealt out. She already understood that, which meant that we had a common ground.

The insomniac in her ensured that she saw plenty of midnight hours, sunrises as she stumbled about, not ready for the next day as each blurred into the next. The cloud of sleep deprivation that bordered onto psychosis in its more intimate moments.

We saw those, too. Stole moments when she slept. Had no idea we were there, inside her space.

And her art. It spoke to both of us in a primitive, prey-in-the-making kind of way.

Because I truly doubted that Helia Mascot was any kind of hunter, even if she would make such a beautiful victim.

"You were never her type," I told Ethan as I bagged his body, careful not to let his blood drain over the flooring in his dorm. His roommate was off fucking another in his frat, and since that particular man had the stamina of a Rippton Allstars, one of the star athletes on campus, I was guaranteed an unbroken handful of hours of sex marathon plus recovery and aftercare time to boot.

His hands and feet were bagged next as I talked to him softly, soothingly.

"She'll be cared for, I promise. No, she doesn't know about the pictures. I'll hide them away," I reassured his head as it went into a plastic bag, separate from the rest of his body. "Unless you *want* her to find them? Did you have a humiliation kink, Art Buddy Ethan? Should I check?"

I raised my eyebrows as blood pooled in the corner of his bag, leaving a soft *plopping* sound as I dropped the dismembered head and bent to collect my blades. I had seven, one of each occasion, though I only used three tonight.

"No, you should not check." My twin brother's voice drew my attention to the window where he balanced in the frame like a moonlit elf.

I imagined that was the filter that Helia would see him through, my pale, pigmentless identical twin. Our albinism was highlighted in the artificial light. Or maybe she wouldn't and I was being a romantic fool, lost in my happy space of murder and death.

"But we could have some fun, message her from his phone," I protested. "I do love games."

"And I love not having to bribe police officers. Don't you remember?" His strict face glowed, forcing me back to the first time I killed. To the memory that set us on the path we followed now.

"Shit. Fuck. I'm—no, I'm not sorry you utter fucking abusive cunt who deserved to die. Shit. Fuck. Fuck!" I gripped my hair in both hands, knowing the stain of my abusive father would transfer to me the moment I grasped the colorless strands and with my bloodied hands and yanked. The pain helped but nothing could alleviate the panic that consumed me as I stared at the fallen body of my sire. The man who decided his son was his toy nightly for years, until I grew old enough to understand what the sharp end of a steak knife could do in a hard grip just after my eleventh birthday.

And already I swore like one of the mafia friends he associated with frequently. I'd sat in on enough meetings, learned the art of negotiation at his table. But I hadn't seen a man bleed so much, hadn't thought it would be so messy when I took the knife and ran it across his throat as he sank his saggy, sloppy body into mine.

And his blood drenched me like a deluge of sin.

The mess was enormous as I managed to haul my skinny, pale ass out from under his convulsing bulk. The scents of death—piss and shit—that I learned to recognize as part of the process later, clung to me that night. Different from any other, a benchmark I lived by from that point.

And as I sat, pointing the steak knife at a still body, covered in another man's blood, Key pushed his way into my room and found me. The knife disappeared from my hand and the body was pulled from the bed. Together, we rolled it and bagged it. And then we phoned one of my father's friends, who turned out not to be a friend at all, but one we could pay to help clean up the mess.

A man who Key had used before.

"Next time, don't be anywhere near the spray," he taught me, showing me how to slash and stab, as I watched, bemused and more than a Little awed at his prowess far greater than my ineptitude. "Watch how they clean up. Ask to help. They'll say no, but they'll let you sit

and observe, providing you don't interrupt. Just watch, and learn. I've been doing it all year."

"Watching?" My eyes were round as saucers, not a shake in sight from my pale, thin hands that my father had loved on his tainted flesh.

Key shook his head, his eyes on the cleaners, absorbing everything.

"Killing."

I hadn't realized what twisted little monsters we were until that moment. Me, out of survival. Him, because he was all sorts of other ways fucked up. I never asked why he was the way he was, simply accepted him. And ... it worked. But my twin still managed to creep up on me sometimes, even when we shared the same obsession.

"Don't fucking well touch anything in his room. Don't gift her anything. Don't *touch her*." Key's personal brand of obsession shone through.

"No?" I traced my fingers across Ethan's sealed lips where I had sewn them shut. "He didn't say much."

Key snorted. "Looking at him now, I don't doubt it."

"Not here. Before." I considered. "It's like...he expected us. Did you make a deal with him?"

Key tilted his head to one side. "No. Did you?"

"I did not."

Breath left me. Why would this man expect us, when we hadn't shown ourselves to Helia yet? Certainly, we'd marked her as ours, but we hadn't shown our obsession, our *dedication* to her to anyone else at all.

"We need to visit her." Key hopped into the room, pacing delicately around my contained crime scene. "This is well done, brother."

I took the rare compliment from him with a nod. "We can touch her? Finally."

His soft laugh left me rock hard in my pants. My natural state during the end of a deal that ended like tonight's has. More than once I've let myself finish over a victim, release the pent up energy. Beau Bennet has been present for several of those occasions as he often feeds our desires. But that little habit is too much, even for the head of the Kingsman fraternity at Rippton U. The college where the country's richest sends their offspring to study, socialize and fornicate while their parents tend to business deals.

Deals that their children would one day replicate, in turn. A closed social infrastructure. It was a hideous net, and by culling the undesirables, I suspect we are simply doing our part. Unfortunately for us, dear old daddy never got to explain his part in the grand scheme, apart from the obvious, and that little habit stops with his grave marker.

"You want to see her? Helia." Key's lips wrapped around our obsession's name like a caress.

I was instantly jealous of his ability to turn that single word into something so much more. "I want to touch her. Tonight. She needs to know us."

Key looked me up and down. "We have a lot of work to do. Cleaning."

"Fine. Only because he pushed too far." I finished tying the head off and double bagged it. Blood had a bad habit of leaking out, especially when the object inside was—ha, pun—a dead weight.

"She was kicked out of her art class tonight." Key let the words out casually.

I blinked. "She was what? Magnus." That man was a bane. I added him to my mental list. Helia was far too decent a talent for his mentorship and that wasn't simply my obsession talking. "What happened?"

Key shrugged and bent to help me with the torso. "He didn't like her sketches. Something inane and cutesy." A grimace curled his lips. "Not her usual, but she earned hate for it. Anyway, they had a fight after you left and she walked out, leaving him holding his limp little dick while the rest of her class watched on."

A warmth started low in my chest. "She owned him," I breathed, suddenly so proud of my girl. Our girl.

Key was right. Helia did Magnus a favor by walking out of his classroom, not in the least because she could now seek a new class to fill her timetable with. But also because while ever I was distracted in following the girl of my literal dreams, then I wasn't in his office, discovering a digit to dismember or another part of his body to damage.

"Indeed." Key directed the rest of the clean up and I took to it, lost in my head. After my shower in the other man's bathroom, and cleaning that too with bleach I didn't need to use, I transferred as much as I expected the bribe to be worth for the local police unit before I called the murder in.

What? I didn't want to keep the parents worrying. There was a responsibility here after all Key disagreed with that last part, not about calling it in but alerting the parents. But if that was my child, I'd want to know.

Not knowing what happened to someone I

loved? That might be the scariest damn thing in the world.

"This is done." Key stretched languorously as flashing lights approached campus. "There. They're coming. Happy now?"

"Immensely." I smiled and shook my head. "The roommate is fucking a few doors up. We should vacate."

He paused, and looked at me. "You want to see her."

I checked the clock tower that sat in the middle of campus. It was well past midnight and I hadn't heard it strike a single hour. "I'll see her whether you're with me, or not."

Key nodded. "Then we go together."

CHAPTER THREE

HELIA

I left my painting on campus, but I kept the concept in my mind. The darkness, the shadows. The blacks and grays. Halfway through painting the new version, I tumbled into bed and passed out. Even my insomnia couldn't fight through the mess of today. Perhaps I should be grateful, but I hated it. Because that simply meant that I'd get a handful of hours of sleep at best and then...the rest of my day would be spent in a literal haze of insomnia fueled brain fog that I wandered about campus in.

And I was already vague and artsy and now I had dropped a class in the middle of semester. I'd be lucky if anyone would take me on, and there was no chance that I was going to call darling daddy like a thousand other girls on campus would do in order to pull a favor.

That wasn't the way my world worked.

As it turned out, I didn't need to make the call. Because the call found me.

I picked it up on the third buzz, my fingers covered in black paint, at a quarter to midnight. That should have been my first clue. The second was the pause before the voice spoke on the other end.

And the final was that anyone called me at all, outside of my regular Taco Tuesday not-date.

"Hello?"

"Helia?"

I spoke over the voice that started talking at the same time that I did, and sighed.

"Dad. Hi." All my energy left me in a rush. "I don't have time for games."

But they're my favorite thing to play.

Once he would have bantered back with me. Now, I only received silence on the other end.

"You're going to get some visitors. I want you to let them in."

I stared at the phone and contemplated telling him where to go. Hanging up. Throw the thing and moving to a different country.

"Why do you care what I do?" Sure, that petulance is the perfect message I want to send back. I picked up my brush and painted.

My hooded man became an invisible monster painted in detail in the shadow. So dark and deep that even I couldn't see him after a while I wondered what else lurked there, created but unseen.

"Helia." My father sighed, as though I had burdened him with a great weight simply in the act of being born. "Help me with his. It's very important for business. I need you to let in the people who I send to you, and do everything that they say. Is that clear?"

I added my teddy in its coffin at the base. Also unseen. Screw Master Magnus. He could go fuck a jar of jelly beans and run off on a sugar high. Damn, I was tired. That was the best insult I had right then.

"Helia, are you listening to me?"

"I'm painting."

"Then stop."

"Paint's fresh."

"Stop."

"It's already been smudged once."

"Stop!"

No.

I'd said it once in the last forty eight hours. I wondered how much more I could say it? But instead, I placed my paint laden fingers on the screen and swiped.

"Good bye, Dad," I said softly.

And kept painting.

A white figure, a wraith or specter I swore I'd seen in my dreams last night flickered in from the edges. When my phone didn't ring again, I threw it onto my bed behind me and kept working. The advantage to living off campus was working my own hours. Not working to dorm hours or roommates. I worked through past midnight, well into the smallest hours, and my specter grew. Taking form from the corner of the canvas where I thought he would stay, this apparition consumed the entire middle of the large rectangular space until it was the centerpiece.

And that's where it stopped. I had no features, only shadows, and so that's what I painted. And painted, until I was done.

And then, I did something I had never done before.

I named it.

CHAPTER FOUR

KEY

Helia Mascot slept. The most hated girl on campus took a brief reprieve in the hours before we became most active, making dark deals and calling out those whose payments fell due.

Tonight, we had no deal to make and sought only one source of vengeance. Tonight, we were a dark dream in the presence of a halo wearing girl.

Only like us, Helia wasn't what she seemed.

Dark hair, raven black, shimmered on her white pillow. Silky ends curled beneath the lace of her flimsy, see through nightie. Dusky shadows and soft peaks interrupted the material's gentle flow where her nipples pressed tight and budded even in her wakeless moments.

Her arms draped softly at her sides as she slept, the lines that marred her face in the daylight hours smoothed in the dark. I slipped my hand across her brow, and she sighed under my touch as though she knew I had come for her.

Like she knew I was there when she shouldn't know any such thing at all.

I froze, torn between wanting her to wake and my desperation for her continued sleep. Because she was so pretty awake, all tortured and shaky and running.

Running from the demons who haunted her across Rippton U's exclusive campus.

She didn't know two devils tracked her panicked footfalls, or what happened to those who made her life hell.

But she would when we let her discover who we were, and why we hunted her.

Our next victim of choice.

We just hadn't decided for what yet. *Our toy.*

My twin trailed his finger along the edge of her covers, drawing the thin sheet down to expose a slice of pale, sweet skin. Unmarked, unmarred.

"So perfect."

"Too perfect."

Kash's pale eyes, hideous in his whitened face

that mirrored mine flicked up to her reddened lips. *Like Snow White but without the touch of innocence.* "Who will mark her first?"

I pressed a hand to his shoulder as his breathing steadied. "We will do this the same way as we do everything."

"Together." His breaths deepened as he watched, grazing his hand above her form, but not quite touching her.

Not yet.

We both craved her fragility with a violence that ran through everything we did, but she was... different.

I nodded. "Together. Let her sleep. The fun is in the hunt."

I watched as he struggled with the concept of walking away from such a tender morsel when she was *right there*. So sweet, not so innocent. So ready to be stripped away, ruined at a moment's notice.

Too perfectly untouched.

That was why we wanted her.

"When?"

"You know when."

"After." His pale hand flexed above her cheek, so close I could almost feel the warmth of her skin though it wasn't my hand that hovered over her alabaster facade.

I nodded, sliding my hand to his chest and pushed once. "For now, we walk away."

She woke one night when I came to see her alone. We didn't often separate, Kash and I, twin brothers working together in almost everything. But a job required a single *soul for a soul* type deal that night, and I couldn't resist her silent siren's call that lured me through the shadows to her room beyond campus grounds.

I kept my distance, trailing my fingers above her skin like he did tonight, touching only the cotton sheet draped over her body to mold into her shape. Her lips parted as she dreamed—no, not dreamed. A nightmare. Soft sounds best befitted to suffering and torture, the sounds I knew so well—those were what slipped from her parted lips.

My cock raged in my leather pants, stiffening until I was fit to burst through the laces that confined me like a cage of her making. Her cries ripped me apart from the insides, a beautiful fucked up torture while she was imprisoned in her head, unable to come out and play.

That was when I touched her. Traced over those

lips, testing the plump softness of them, how easily she yielded to me.

And when I slid first one, then two fingers inside her warm, wet mouth, she closed those tempting lips around my intrusion and sucked gently on my fingers, her sounds became something else entirely.

Had I been with my brother, it wouldn't have been my fingers she sucked.

But I didn't want to rob him of that first. And so when she woke, I lingered long enough to memorize her dozy confusion. Her dark eyes remained unfocused as she stared at me, murmuring a word I nearly missed.

Seraph.

And now, a life sized painting of a glowing white form existed in the darkness of her room, warding away demonic forms, looking over her as she slept.

Like we did.

An obsession indeed.

Kash leaned forward, pushing his resistance into my hand until my nails dug into his skin beneath his silk shirt. I'd make him bleed on this, if I had to, and he would bleed for her willingly as would I.

Instead, he inhaled her, his nose skimming the air above her skin, his tongue flickering out to taste the remnants of her dream.

"Tomorrow."

I smiled, and we melted into the shadows as she stirred, the twin seraph she painted, winging away as we protected her from afar.

Only we weren't angels watching over her but the worst of nightmares come to claim what would be ours.

CHAPTER FIVE

HELIA

"Can you see him? Anything that looks like him?" Angelica's voice spoke in my ear like some kind of undercover operative in a spy movie.

But we weren't playing spies and heroes tonight. Nope, it was Tuesday night. Death Date Night, or Death to Dating Night. Cheap night at plenty of bars, pizzerias, and diners.

Also Taco Tuesday, and I was missing out.

The night I tried to become Tinderella for the tenth consecutive week in a row.

And my tenth epic fail, also consecutive.

"That's it. I'm done." I shrugged, downed my water in a tumbler to make it look like vodka because I didn't want to be sad and alone, despite how I felt.

"Stay another five minutes," Angelica urged. "You know I live vicariously through you. Give me that."

"Uh huh. And how is that facade of life going for you right now?" I snorted into my glass, talking to myself.

I mean, how sad could I possibly look? My strike rate so far wasn't particularly hot, sizzling, or even flopping.

Six stand ups, and four half shows of the '*my mother is dying and I have to leave*' hurrying off variety.

It was like no man on Rippton U's wealthy offspring inhabited campus would come within sneezing distance of me. I might as well have a sign that proclaimed '*anathema*' stamped to the top of my head for all and sundry to see.

Angelica rattled on, impervious to my moods, as always. "I get to pretend to leave my apartment, sit in a cafe, and sip water, all whilst *not* infecting the local area with my hyperactivity, or my crippling anxiety. You know, whichever lands first."

"I think you get the better part of this deal," I

said dryly. "Alright. His time is up. It's been forty minutes. Enough is enough."

"Oh, girl. Go flirt with the bartender."

"It's a girl."

"So? Go get laid. A change of pace never hurt."

Yeah, but there is no pace, and no one is getting laid.

"You mean the diner server?" I eyed said waitress who winked at me, letting a quick fantasy play out in my head. A moment later my glass wasn't the only damp thing about the table.

The little diner just outside campus limits was still a favorite haunt for locals and students alike. A presence that all the wealth in the kingdom wasn't indeed theirs, and that they could live a normal life, offspring of billionaires all of them.

cough us *cough*

More fakeness and bullshit.

I bought into it just like everyone else.

"Um, yeah," Angelica replied sheepishly.

"Girl in the chair, thank you for spending another amazing Tuesday Not Date Night with yours truly."

"Talk to you next week, sister." Angelica sent air kisses and signed off.

I pulled the earpiece out, turned it over and

dropped the tiny miracle of technology into my black glitter purse, the item totally out of place in the white and red splashed retro themed milkshake bar-cum-diner that served alcohol after ten P.M.

The bell over the door tinkled. I craned my neck to watch who came in, praying it wasn't my late date now that I'd made my choice to go the hell home.

Two tired cops on their local beat, each grumpier looking than the last, entered the diner, marring the colorful facade with their gritty noir darkness which made it my cue to *really* leave.

Date Night is done for another week.

"Fuck me, my life is sad," I muttered, finishing my water.

"You want a coffee to go, sweetie?" The waitress appeared at my table on cue.

"Thanks, Misha. Appreciate you." I made a heart with my hands and she ruffled my hair.

"I won't be a minute, date girl."

She didn't lie; in less than sixty seconds I clutched a tall, black, burned coffee that singed my insides and clung to them like so much ash as I made the diner door tinkle on my way out, waving to my regular waitress.

"Sooo sad," I sang to the night air, scaring a sleeping quail that hightailed it along the dimly lit path I took, darting side to side in a flurry like a suicide chicken as it assumed I chose to chase it.

Run, run, birdie.

I giggled at the tiny creature's antics as it veered off the path and disappeared beneath a bush. A pair of luminous, disembodied eyes peered back at me.

"Night night, cutie."

I blew the quivering quail a kiss, and turned off at the next fork away from campus and the lecture halls at the exclusive, rich kid and legacy alumni admissions only college.

Rippton wasn't a place where I thought I'd spend my newly found freedom, but my parents paid the tithes to be rid of the only child they never seemed to want seeing as I didn't fit into their *perfect progeny* mould while I inherited a boatload of abandonment issues and an apartment of my choice on the edge of town.

Sororities and parties never did it for me. Perching on my window seat, a glass of red wine dangling from my hand as I watched the college town grow silent each night, leaving me with the taste of dew on the icy night air, though? That did.

The same air that drifted through the arched floor to ceiling window I left open every night that was big enough for an adult to easily step through if they were willing to risk their existence over a sheer, four-story drop to the filthy streetscape below.

The nights I left my window open were the nights I slept best, as though the soft murmur of the sleepy town's night time comings and goings filtered through to me in my dreamstate like a conversation I could listen to but didn't have to engage in.

Hell, I'd even woken once from a dream to find a glowy, white angel standing at the end of my bed. Lost in a dream? Maybe. Cliche, but true. It took a few blinks for him to disappear, but my comfort level rose, and I clung to that pretense that all was right in the world, and that good girls went to heaven.

Not that I'd ever been the epitome of one of those, but I could pretend on that basis too.

Anyone else might freak out, but my weird happy zone appeared to be the reverse of everyone else's.

Everyone, except maybe Angelica.

The blonde anxiety bomb of a hermit rarely ventured from her apartment. Everything was ordered in, including her online classes. Thanks to her family's—wealthy—intervention, she got to study as she liked, providing she kept her marks up. Angelica was no party girl risk, and her grades never fell below a high distinction level, leaving her exactly where she wanted to be—alone.

I sipped my scalding, ashy coffee, twisted my way through the streets, and took as many different options as possible.

Angelica, your paranoia is infectious.

Just as her laughter and cheeky sense of humor that no one ever saw was contagious. It was sad, really. She was such a beautiful person, and kept it all to herself. But, preferences, and I was glad I had one commiserator in this weird little existence until I was freed from both Rippton and my family's ever-present expectations.

I laughed to myself, snuggling the warmth of my tall take away cup to my chest. The streets behind the rows of shops were silent, save for the light drizzle of rain that stopped and started on a whim. Townhouses and narrow residential alleyways turned into gritty lanes filled with rubbish of mechanics shops and commercial properties.

Somewhere behind me, tin banged on tin, the sound reverberating along the narrow light industrial street.

I quickened my steps, pushing my pace ever faster until I came to a corner, and picked the path back to suburbia. Which would have been a solid strategy on any other night, barring not-date-night, anti-Taco Tuesday.

Tonight, my choices led me straight into the arms of devils.

I barreled around the next corner, head down, hell bent on getting home to my apartment out of the rain, sending Angelica a message stating how she'd skewed my sense of everything when I slammed head first into a solid something that unfortunately for both of us wore my burnt coffee.

"Damn, I was enjoying that." I looked up, my apology on my lips. "I'm sorry. I wasn't–"

I kept looking up. And up, and up.

Right into the face of an angel.

If angels were monstrous creatures born of pale skin, white hair so fine the moonlight left traces of celestial dust on each strand, and palest blue eyes highlighted with a sliver of demonic red.

This one stood at least six and a half feet tall, with broad shoulders, and felt like steel to run face first into.

He also wore my coffee.

"I'm so sorry," I whispered, reaching out to—pat him dry, try to wipe the mess away—but his expression stopped me.

Disgust.

"Oh. Um, I hope that comes out. I'll just be—"

A second angel appeared slightly behind the first, as close to identical as my artist's eye could tell in the dark night, despite the starlight tracing their sharp features made for demons and put in the wrong body.

I twisted back, *knowing* my instinct served me wrong, only inciting the predators lurking within those beautiful bodies, and stopped, already face to nipple height with the next. The first turned on his heel in a delicate as fuck pivot better suited to a dance floor than an alley I should never have set foot in, sandwiching me between their bodies, effectively blocking my path.

I bit my lip, edging sideways. They came too, reducing my exit options to exactly zilch.

The second angel raised his hand, stroking a slicked finger across my cheek. "She's so much prettier when she's awake. I thought it was the other way around."

"Much prettier," the first agreed. "Especially with the addition of blood." A cool hand caught my chin, tilting my head back from behind me so the angel-demon there could stare into my upside down eyes.

I blinked, recognized the features I tried so hard to wash away with my wakefulness as the truth I tried so hard to ignore and deny in my waking hours slammed into me.

"I painted you. My angel," I blurted. "My seraph." That last came out on a whisper. A breath.

A confession.

CHAPTER SIX

KASH

Recognition flared in her eyes, and I smiled. Not something I did often, but with Helia, I couldn't help the emotions that ran riot through me, unchecked. A dangerous ripple of energy flowed through me, echoing in my brother. His body tensed, and I knew he felt it too. *Her.*

My twin and I stalked our little toy for the past semester, warning away every male who looked at her with lustful eyes, desire written across their faces as they studied her lithe wisp of a body, the hand that strayed to rub their hardening cocks when they thought she wasn't looking.

But we were, so often to their detriment.

She rarely ate, preferring it seemed to fast,

though she was as wealthy as any student on campus. Helia also preferred to live off site, a choice that bemused and interested me.

Everything about her was curious, like a modern Alice prepared to tumble down her chosen rabbit hole.

Or perhaps we chose the rabbit hole for her.

"We saw your painting," I murmured, spreading around the blood my twin swiped across her skin, marring her innocence and marking her at once.

He took the first honors.

I supposed I should be mad. Helia had been our obsession, obscuring every aspect of our business with her curious little life, so much that we completed tonight's work on her behalf without realising we stood in her path. Her surprise encounter of us was a door that swung both ways.

A gift, perhaps. A strand of fate intertwined with ours.

And yet we were drawn together like so many satellites orbiting a greater mass that drew us into her with a force much heavier than gravity.

This tiny slip of a girl who consumed me.

I swallowed, letting my heavy gaze drop to her lips. "Open your mouth."

"What? Why?" Confusion swirled in the shadowed eddies of her eyes, though something flickered in their tumultuous depths that reeled me in like a singularity I couldn't escape.

"I want to know if you taste like innocence or sin," I whispered, sliding my nose along her cheek, inhaling her.

My brother stood on her other side, blocking her path, his breaths even as always. I could take my time with my seduction.

Usually a job—like tonight's—involving metal and blood, and the end of things signaled a night of cleaning up, a conclusion of playtime. But Helia— she was a beginning.

I didn't know of what, and that made me curious. Like her.

She didn't pull away, that inquisitive nature drawing her into me as I fell into her in return. Like suicide.

And with my brother watching on, his desire hidden beneath layers of forced dispassion, I lowered my mouth to brush over, around hers, and slid my tongue inside the wet corners of her lips.

Starlight and first rain, desperation and acquiescence.

That's what she tasted like as I increased the pressure of my lips on hers, sealing our mouths together. She flinched before her body softened, a moment of *fight or flight* response kicking in as I stole her air, luring her soul closer to mine.

One kiss, and the need to possess every inch of her consumed me.

Key's hands slid around her waist, pulling her sharply back, breaking the moment.

"Share her, brother," he murmured.

His blood stained fingers trailed along her cheek as he tilted her head back and replaced my mouth with his on her soft lips. Those fingers slipped fluidly over her decolletage until he left traces of scarlet and sin around her breast, circling her taut nipples through her shirt.

She writhed slightly in his hold, but unlike my featherlight touch, he crushed her against him, devouring her mouth with a ravenous hunger.

I groaned low in my throat as she arched, thrusting her tits into my waiting hands. Knocking Key's away, I cupped her breasts, rolling the nipples through the delicate fabric of her blouse beneath her leather jacket. I was desperate to feel her bare beneath me. We both were. The tease had gone on for weeks.

Now we had her...I didn't want to rush, unwrapping each layer of the present she made of herself, falling into us during the darkest hours, letting us touch her while covered with the lifeblood of another.

Her soft whimpers pulled me out of my head. Breathing hard, like I was the one with my mouth smashed to hers, I tugged her nipples, alternating pinches and barely there touches until she was torn between us, shattering and reforming the way we created her.

Finally, Key lifted his head, his pinkish-pale gray eyes that matched mine locking onto me. "We take her home."

And she will never leave.

He wanted to cage her, use her body endlessly, keep her in a teased and tortured place where their minds melded. The idea was appealing, I had to admit. Having her there to toy with whenever the need to possess her arose.

But the desire we built our obsession on came from her freedom. Her ability to run...or not.

The chase, even if she didn't know we were there.

"Her place," I murmured into the hollow of her throat. "Fuck her, coat her in ourselves, and leave her there, aching and moaning for us. Which we will come back to give to you," I promised her. "Our little Alice."

"What?" Helia gasped softly as the air she needed filled her lungs, her chest expanding beneath my hands. "You– who are you two?"

"Apart from the angels who watch you sleep?" Key mocked.

"We could have filled that little mouth so many times," I murmured, catching Key's hand with its remnants of a once life that was never intended for her, and lifted his fingers to her lips. "Suck."

Helia's lips closed around his digits, her eyes widening as the taste registered. Her head shook side to side, but I held her face still while she cried sweet tears for me.

"Don't you know what we are?" Key asked softly in her ear, caressing her lips as she fought us.

"Haven't you listened to the stories on campus?" I murmured, licking the corners of her mouth where her lips stretched around my twin's fingers, collecting the remnants of her tears, her horror.

He slipped another in, fucking her mouth slowly, relentlessly.

Helia mumbled an answer around the intrusion, her words too muffled to make out. I nodded and Key removed his fingers, letting her breathe again. Saliva dribbled down her chin, dripping wet spots onto her blouse until the outline of her breasts with no bra was clearly visible, the tight peaks of her nipples pushing against the red stained material, evidence of our insanity and our lust.

"You're Key and Kash," she whispered, her gaze darting between us, framed by flushed cheeks. "The psyc–" She coughed. "The twins."

"Yes," I murmured.

Her brow dipped, like she expected more. A lie, perhaps.

"I don't speak to many people," she choked out. "I have hardly any friends."

I smiled, brushing her cheek with the backs of my scarred knuckles. "We know, little Alice. We made you anathema to the student population...and other places. Didn't you wonder why date night never happened?"

Her eyes flared white. "You...left me alone?"

A soft laugh broke painfully from my chest. "Yes, and no. We are always with you. In classes, when you sleep." I brushed my thumb across her bottom lip, giving only the slightest pressure, but she opened for me.

My smile widened, my predator's need to rip her clothes apart and fuck her there in the gravel on the side of the street building in my heart. I turned my hand on her cheek, giving into the urge that drove me, and gripped her face hard.

Her soft cry rippled through the night air as I forced her to look deep into the tight alleyway between the last of the commercial buildings on the block before the houses started.

"See." Key caressed the shell of her ear with his tongue, laving the sensitive areas as she shook in our hold. "He wasn't good enough to touch you, little Alice."

"Stop calling me that." She swept a hand back, touching us for the first time, cupping my brother's cheek like a long time lover.

Key's groan echoed her cry of a moment before in the stillness, and her eyes drifted shut. The corners of her lip turned up in a secret smile that left my cock straining to slide into her mouth and fuck her tight throat until she choked on me, dressed me in her tears and saliva.

"See," I repeated firmly, tapping her cheek.

Helia's eyes drifted open, focusing on the alleyway where I directed her.

That sumptuous mouth fell open, the tip of her pink tongue straying out though her hand stayed on my brother's cheek as she froze, taking in the dismembered body missing both its hands.

Her fingers traveled to her lips, rubbing thought-fully across them. "Is that...?"

"Your date for tonight," Key whispered. "He planned to bring you home, fuck you, and throw you out onto the streets for his gang friends to use later. He defiled a picture he printed out of you from your dating profile with his worthless seed."

"We couldn't have that." I shrugged, but pulled her closer. "The disrespect, that he thought you were so much trash to throw away."

"He wasn't worthy to fuck your sweet body."

"And he didn't want to keep you."

"So we removed the choice of his poisonous intent and replaced it with pain," Key finished his epitaph.

Her head swiveled between us, her hand dropping slightly. I sucked in the breath she let out, savoring the air like it was my last. My little Alice held my gaze, watchful, unmoving.

"You did this for me?"

Key caught her wrist, pressing a brutal kiss there, biting her skin hard enough to mark but not break her flesh, then licked the inside of her palm soothingly. Her fingers curled up, tracing the archer's bow of his lips that mirrored mine. I touched my own mouth, moaning at the caress I *almost* felt first hand as her breath hitched.

"He was going to throw me away for others to rape?" she whispered, staring between us, understanding *finally* what we did for her.

What we had done for the past weeks. Horror stretched her stunning, ethereal features, and her deep breaths came shallow and short as she swayed between us on unsteady feet.

I clasped her face between my cold hands, her heat warming me from the outside in. "He was. But we prevented that, and now you are here with us." My words were fierce, the light in my eyes more than obsessive.

I knew what I looked like as the same light was reflected in my brother's face, like rapture as I watched her face intently, knowing her choice in this moment was the one that would define her future.

A cage, like Key wanted.

Freedom, and be hunted to appease my devil.

She held my gaze and pressed forward until her lips brushed mine.

"Thank you," she whispered.

CHAPTER SEVEN

HELIA

My breath shuddered in the infinitely minute space between our lips. Kash froze, his strange, almost purple eyes in the odd lighting between night and faintly reflected street light boring through me. Rainwater dripped down his cheek, streaking the blood spattered across his pale flesh.

A breath. That's all the reprieve I earned from their hunger before his mouth slammed into mine, crushing my body between theirs.

Fingers and hands that belonged to both of them wandered over my skin, their dual touch sweet and discovering at first but quickly devolving into gripping and tearing. The twins snarled over my flesh, sucking and licking and biting.

My body ached between them, months of forced deprivation–from *them,* because of *them*–bereft of touch and contact with any other human, anyone at all, left me a needy mess, desperate for anything they offered.

They killed for me.

A sacrifice gifted me on an altar of gravel and shattered glass.

The thought should have been abhorrent. I should have run screaming from them, ripped my hands from their grasp, found the nearest safe house and phone, and dialed 911.

I did nothing like that.

The strange thing about attending Rippton U was that we were all the same. Our families were wealthy enough to bend any law, hell, even break them. Sad to say, I could count my own parents in that quarter. This wasn't my first body.

That happened when I was ten years old, prepubescent and crushing on Randy Grower, the boy of the moment in the fifth grade. I came home, hoping for one of Mom's special hot chocolates and a goss sesh. Instead, I found myself holding plastic garbage bags, with oversized rubber gloves to my armpits, playing a macabre version of Tetris with human limbs as my mother hacked away on the kitchen floor, identity forever unknown because it didn't matter.

I earned my special hot chocolate that day for the first time.

And many times after.

The knowledge I was about to be fucked between a pair of psychotic albino identical twins with a killer habit wasn't such a far stretch.

My seraphs.

Key—or Kash, I couldn't tell their touches apart when they were both as desperate in their roughened caresses as they made me—ripped my shirt from neckline to hem, shredding the thin fabric and lowered his mouth to my bare nipples.

Every bite and lick lifted me higher, the ache between my thighs intensifying.

As though reading my mind, he dropped his hands between my legs, clawing at my panties. One long finger stroked between his frenzied grasp from behind, and my breath stalled in my throat. Kash took the opportunity to capture my jaw in those long, knowing fingers, tilting my head back as he had when he bruised my mouth perfectly a moment before.

I'm as broken as they are.

Maybe not quite as twisted. But my head liked

that they killed for me. What better profession of...
love? Desire?...could a girl want?

Their words. Their touch.

And as they ripped me apart, they did just that.

Kash licked my lips, holding his mouth over mine. A thin stream of spit dribbled into my mouth as they played with my pussy, tugging and pulling roughly, stroking firmly. I squeezed my thighs together against the insistent ache, but Key tapped my cheek.

"Open," he said firmly, prying my jaw wide as feet tapped my legs apart.

"Swallow." Kash plunged two fingers inside me the moment I obeyed the command.

They swapped places and I cried into Key's mouth, their touch melding again as he worked a finger inside me along with his brother's.

The sensation of having two demanding lovers play with me at once was like nothing I'd ever experienced. Pressure increased within me as one finger curled to torture the inside of my walls at the sensitive spot behind my belly, the others thrusting in and out at a punishing pace my over sensitized body couldn't compete with.

"Is this how you fuck, too?" I gasped, arching into the dual touch, hovering somewhere between the edge of my orgasm and falling off an unseen precipice.

Don't let me fall.

Please catch me.

"You want us together?" one twin murmured into my mouth.

I nodded with my eyes closed, unsure who I kissed.

"Like this?"

I suffered the insertion of another finger inside my slit, my arousal coating us all as they moved in tandem, stroking inside me, working with, then against each other. I wondered who would be the first to get off if those fingers were cocks. That erotic thought of the brothers spilling their cum bare in my pussy and coating my thighs broke me.

The shudders came first, then a scream one of them swallowed, both men grinding hard against me, pinning me between unyielding bodies. The heel of a hand slammed over my clit, setting off a second round of pulses that overtook me. I bore down, my legs giving out with the intensity of plea-sure that consumed me.

"That's it, pretty Alice," Kash murmured.

"Fuck our fingers," Key encouraged.

They worked harder, my orgasm never ending,

until I opened my eyes and stared up at the stars between the utilitarian buildings. A slice of beauty, diamonds set in midnight velvet surrounded by the hardness of ruined life below.

I floated between them, my legs wrapped around Key's waist. They'd turned me around, my back pressed to Kash's hard chest as they bore my body like I weighed nothing.

Pressure built in my pussy, stretching and tugging. I stared down between us as one of the boys held both their cocks in a white knuckled grip, pushing their purple, straining heads into me. A scream built in my throat, but it never had the chance to escape.

A hand identical to the one forcing their cocks inside my engorged, slicked flesh cupped over my mouth. The fingers caressed the corners of my mouth gently, teasing them while he suffocated me.

"Lie back," Key murmured the command, the hand shifting to make room for him to brush his lips back and forth over mine.

I sucked in shuddering breaths as tears slipped from the corners of my eyes, and licked someone's tongue as my pussy stretched and they filled me.

Owned me.

"Let us take care of you."

The hand holding my mouth shifted, squeezing until I opened. A tongue slipped inside, searching languidly. An erotic, knowing touch so different to the rough way they manhandled me that I came on the spot.

Hot liquid squirted down my legs, coating their cocks and balls with my obscene deluge of need.

The mouth against mine smiled, cold and calculating. "Perfect."

Two cocks slammed together inside me, the hand at my mouth dropping to my throat and cutting off my air. Killing my scream.

Not taking a second for me to recover or become used to the invasive stretch, they began to move in tandem, fucking me at the same time like a giant cock, thick and impaling, moving as one.

My traitorous body aided them, more of my cum dripping from the hole they sealed with their obsessive desire for my body.

For me.

A long, breathless moan lodged behind the hand holding my throat.

"You won't get air, little Alice." A twin sucked on my ear lobe, twirling his tongue over my flesh like it was my nipple, or my clit.

My pussy contracted hard, my hips rolling forward, a compulsion drawn out of my control.

"Oh, how she does like to be sucked and licked," the other twin whispered.

I moaned silently, milking their offering that sliced through me. Their hips jerked together until their combined monster cock threatened to split me.

A single tear trickled along my cheek as I opened my mouth for the kiss pressed there. The salty drop was licked away, accompanied by a deep groan. That I had the power to make the manic twins need me to the point of our mutual destruction brought me to the edge of my orgasm a third time. Hands dropped to my hips as I clenched down, and their movements changed.

One twin fucked in, and the other slid out of my drenched hole. They reversed the motion like an efficient machine, fucking into my stretched pussy until my head dropped back, my body softening. I screamed silently into the quiet nightscape, punctuated by their huffs and moans. Hands bruised my body, tenderizing me like so much meat to be consumed.

Perhaps that's all I was to the two angels ruining a mortal in the rain beside a life already stolen. I came hard at the dual invasion, their brutality too much for my over sensitized body to handle, clenching down and strangling their cocks with my walls.

You are mine.

Both of you.

I whispered the words to the midnight sky as their hands tightened, bodies stiffening. Their last few thrusts bordered on painful, insanity gripping them greater than before, bleeding into me.

And we fell into the stars together.

CHAPTER EIGHT

KEY

I stared down at the sleeping angel in her bed, still covered in her date's blood, her thighs glistening with our personal brand of depravity. My cock ached from working her vice-like pussy. Every part of me throbbed, but not as bad as she would come sunrise when we were gone. Already the evidence of our violence covered her skin in marks that bloomed, a trail of torture she'd remember in the morning.

Would she run and scream then, let us chase her? Let us cage her? One fantasy melded into the next, more fucked up that the previous one. We wanted them all.

My balls refilled at the thought of fucking that pretty little mouth in her bed like I always planned, sliding in and out of her pretty lips and drowning her mouth in my come. Letting her sleep in a puddle, wake to the tainted taste of me in her mouth, on her precious, sullied lips.

Now she was ours there was little to stop me from making good on my promise to myself.

To the one I made to her.

When we brought her back to her apartment we slid the tattered blouse and rumpled skirt from her exhausted body but she was already out, leaning her weight on us. I untied her boots while my brother redressed her in her lace nightie, leaving her covered in the fluids of tonight's obsession, of course.

She loved when we marked her; I saw that in her eyes when my brother bit and sucked on her throat. When my fingers dug into her hips, leaving perfect bruises there to remind her of who owned her.

We played nicely with her for this round.

She would remain free, and we would watch her, hunt her.

A catch and release scheme, if only for now.

But still as I stared down at her, something was missing.

I glanced to my side where Kash undid his belt, sliding his hardened cock into his hand. His smile was depraved, lacking love. Glowing with need and obsession.

"Once more," he whispered into the darkened room, standing above her.

And to the memory of her cries as we fucked her innocence away, we emptied our balls over her sleeping figure, coating her hair and lips with pearlescent strands. Our cum dripped into her parted lips, and she swallowed reflexively in her sleep.

"Perfect." I trailed my fingers along her arm, sighing when she pulled my hand into her chest, snuggling. Her heart beat against the heightened pulse in my fingers, claiming me.

My heart hitched at the thought she wanted us, *needed* us to stay with her.

But not tonight.

Kash played with her feet, running his fingertips along her soles until she made soft noises. I dragged the low easel with her life sized angel portrait to the end of her bed, leaving the static seraph to watch over her in place of us while we worked for the rest of the night.

There were still two more dates to remove from her list before we deleted her from social media. Her presence would cease to exist, one shred at a time, until we took her.

Until she was ours in full, and came to us willingly.

She might now, but there would always remain a doubt. Helia would run and hide, and we would chase.

All willingly....and sometimes not so.

And we would shatter her, remake her as we saw fit.

Then, at the end of our games, she would come to us.

Until then...I kissed her temple. "Sleep well, little Alice," I whispered, licking her skin. "I'll watch you every night so you can sleep. The demons will never touch you. I promise. We will protect you, forever."

Because the devils watched over her.

Helia shifted, stirring as I held my breath.

In her sleep, she smiled, whispered a word.

"Forever."

CHAPTER NINE

HELIA

They called me Little Alice and I loved it. I also knew I was in over my head by a long way. The twins followed me everywhere. Even when they thought they couldn't see me, or I thought I was alone, I'd turn a corner and one of them would be there, waiting to shadow me to class. Not that we had a normal relationship, like holding hands and being romantic—because why would we do that when they killed a man just to date me?

Taco Tuesday was officially a bust and Angelica faded back into her own routine of no people and her own life of study. I couldn't draw her out of it, and so I merged my life with the twins. Because they were there? Maybe. Because I owned them? Absolutely.

Should the murder have bothered me more? I mean, I came from a family that revolved around underhand bargains struck at tables across the country. I still wasn't sure what my father wanted the night he called but I was glad that insanity had passed. The twins weren't really a stretch from that place in my life. Hell, if I introduced them to Dad, he'd probably approve of them—if he knew what they did, and how well.

"This isn't the best place to accost me," I protested, as Kash gripped my elbow through my faded denim jacket.

I'd worn it over my black singlet t-shirt dress today with lace straps as it looked like rain earlier, but I hadn't been outside in hours, hoping from art history class to a digital and new media lecture that I'd thought I would hate at the beginning of semester but ended up loving.

They'd left me alone for the better part of today, and I should have known better than to expect solitude altogether.

"I do get to have days to myself, you know–oh, fuck," I cursed as Kash dragged me from the building into the pelting rain without a second's hesitation. "I could have art that's getting damaged, you know!"

He cast me a quick, hard look over his shoulder that pierced right through me.

"So, run."

I took the hint as he gripped my hand firmly—there's that stupid, romantic notion again—and darted after him, gripping the strap on my shoulder satchel as hard as I could as I put my head down, trusted that he knew where he was going, and blindly ran.

By the time that we reached our destination. I swore that he had picked the longest route possible, halfway across campus through the rain instead of dashing from building to building to seek shelter. I stared at the almost skeletal looking man before me. Pale, pigmentless hair plastered to his head, and pinkish eyes stared at me from an angular face. His white shirt clung to every plane of his hard body, and there were plenty of those. Kash stalked toward me, breathing hard as he backed me toward a sandstone alcove.

"Where are we?" I asked as a distraction.

The clock above me in its tower struck the hour, dead on time in its answer, drowning out my next words, and any of his, though as usual the twin before me wasn't terribly talkative.

His hand rose to catch my jaw in hard grip, and then his mouth crashed down on mine.

I whispered, straining up to meet him, seeking warmth in his kiss even as I pulled back, pressing away from him, deeper into the sandstone. His laugh against my mouth was broken as he caged me in and leaned his cold, wet body against mine. Damp clothes tangled as he itched my dress up, and pressed a knee between my legs.

Material wrapped around limbs where it shouldn't be, trapping me in place. I struggled when he shoved my jacket over my shoulders, punning my arms by my sides.

"This isn't fair," I managed. "You're far too organized for me."

The flicker of metal and dull light together glinted, and my scream jammed in my throat as his blade pressed between my breasts.

Kash watched my face carefully. "Key promises me that you're made for us, little Alice. That you understand why we stole lives for you. Do you?" he waggled the blade across the tops of my breasts, until I moaned for him.

"That— that—" I managed as the flat of the blade produced sensations over my skin that I'd never felt before. I sighed, and leaned into him, letting the blade dig in. "It's good."

"Isn't it?" he agreed, humming softly, low in his throat. The blade flicked to the sides, once, then twice. And my wet dress fell away, exposing my breasts.

I should have been shocked or cried out, but I arched instead, wanting his hands on me, knowing his touch would be freezing after our run through the rain.

"Please," I begged, and I swore his eyes narrowed.

Kash turned away, gripping my hand and tossed me away from the wall, toward a set of stairs. I climbed them behind him, my dress clutched in one hand, my other laced in his, though I didn't dare cover up. When we reached the top landing, I found myself in an open plan bedroom, split in two sides.

Two identities. My Seraphs.

One covered in books, the other in computer equipment.

"You live behind the clock, don't you?" I clutched my ruined dress and Kash's hand, unwilling to let either go.

And in one cover, sat the smudged board that I had left in David Magnus's studio that he promised to hide behind the rest of his old student's works and leave to dust and obscurity.

"You saved it," I whispered in awe.

"I saved it."

Key stepped out of the shadows behind us, and pushed the door shut. It slammed, its echo filtering down the endless stairwell.

"Thank you," I whispered.

Key's sharp gaze drifted between his twin's hand and my sliced duress, then nodded. "It's only us."

I sucked in a splintered breath, and looked up at Kash to find an identical hungry look on his angular, striking face.

"Let us see you, Helia," he murmured. One hand drifted up to graze the side of my breast.

Pleasure ricocheted through me, and between my legs heated, slicking. I knew if they touched me there, they *know*.

"Why me?" I asked, knotting my dress between my breasts. Knowing they could see everything, letting them drink in everything.

Key focused on my face. "Because you see the world with a clarity others lack. In your art, in how you talk to people."

I remembered my conversation with my father. "If you asked my dad, you might change your opinion of me," I muttered, pulling my dress up, suddenly feeling unworthy of his assessment.

Kash's grip at my waist yanked me into him. My dress tugged away to pool at his fingers, and then there was no recovering it. "I'll tell you a story about my father, wraith." His mouth brushed over mine. "When I was a child he used to rape me. He used to abuse me and use me nightly. Do you know what I did to him?"

I held his gaze because I knew he needed it. "You killed him."

"I killed him." He licked the corners of my lips as his fingers glided to my nipples, toying with them. I arched backward and butted my head into Key's shoulder. A cry tore from me, and he admonished me.

"Shh. Listen, Little Alice. Hear my brother."

Kash stroked my breasts, tracing along the undersides as I sighed and panted for him. "I learned the value of taking a life, and the pleasure it gave me. What I could do for those I love. I learned how to protect the woman that I love." He put his hand into his back pocket as Key growled, and I had the impression that he didn't approve of this next part. But Kash did it anyway, placing a stack of photos into my hands.

I flicked through, unsure what I looked at, then back at them both.

"These are from your art buddy's room. He thought that taking pictures of you then jerking off over them would be good fun," Key murmured in my ear as he toyed with my breasts. One hand curled around my throat and she squeezed rhythmically. "Would you approve?"

I stared at the pictures of me naked, in my bed, in my shower. In my home.

And I knew the answer.

"Only if it was you." I twisted to stare at him, then at Kash. "Or you."

The sounds they made, as contemplated Ethan's absence, and what that meant, were primal and perfect. Their bodies rubbed against mine as mouths descended on mine, my lips, my throat, my breasts, licking and sucking and invading.

"On the bed."

The order came from someone, and they lifted me. I found myself stretched across a wide bed, my legs pressed together as one twin positioned himself behind me, working his cock into my closed pussy. I moaned at the sensation, though the arm that banded around my stomach left me hot and flushed.

"Little Alice likes being held down," Key murmured—from behind me, I realized.

"Not half as much as she likes being fucked when she's asleep." This from Kash.

It took a full minute for those words to penetrate my sex hazed mind as Key shoved his cock inside my drenched pussy. He groaned at the same time as I screeched, *"What?"*

Key's laugh as he lay behind me on his side, with me completely impaled on his cock, might have been the most erotic thing I'd ever done.

Until his hand wrapped around my throat a second time—gently this time— as he leaned in. "Lie still, like a doll, and we'll show you what we like to do to you while you sleep, Helia. Once we fucked you. Sometimes we just come on you. And other times, we come in your mouth. You're so stunning and soft and responsive in your sleep." His cock kicked in my pussy and I moaned.

Kash pulled aside the rest of my dress and latched his mouth over my clit, sucking and licking like he was Frenching my mouth, only he wasn't....and it was my pussy instead.

I came almost instantly, milking Key's cock to the music of his groans.

"Fuck, yes. Just like that, doll. You're perfect," he

praised me. "In your sleep you come easily too. One day we'll video you so you can see the things we do to you."

I choked behind his hand as Kash continued his teasing kisses on my pussy. "Should he stop," I managed to gasp in enough breath, rocking my hips to and from twin to twin.

"Ohh, fuck," Key muttered as I rocked on him. "Wraith, we can't have that. So either you crash his face and he still licks you, or you hold still while he makes you orgasm and he drives himself to you today. And me? I'm going to stretch this pretty cunt and cum inside you soon."

I whimpered and forced myself to hold still, raking my fingers along Key's thigh as I came again for cock and tongue.

And neither of them seemed to mind.

CHAPTER TEN

KEY

Helia agreed to attend a frat party on a leash. She might be the single prettiest, most addictive sight I'd ever seen, and she was attached to my wrist as I towed her along behind me. Kash, of course, brought up the rear—no one was allowed to touch her but us. He talked to her softly, his voice too low for me to hear. I wasn't sure if he whispered secrets to her that left her dripping, or praised her for being so good for us.

Either way, her presence left me on edge from the way she behaves for us. Too good. Too perfect. Like this was how she's meant to be by design, and not ours.

I tugged on the leash a little harder. She stumbled forward to the music of Kash's laughter, and some of the boys drinking around us. Naturally, in her stockings and mini dress—black, of course to our pale suits and white shirts, she drew a crowd. Or perhaps, we do.

Spinning on my heel, I stalked back toward her, meeting her halfway as she stumbled into me. Our mouths clashed together in a collision of teeth and lips and tongue. Helia softened in my arms until I let her go, throwing her backward. Kash caught her easily, but the hurt in her eyes was unmistakable. She didn't know what she'd done wrong, and I couldn't explain that it was my fault. I shouldn't have put her on display, and now that we're out, I coulnd't drag her back to our room and fuck her without completing the night first.

And so she'd have to wear my ire until we were done.

I thought that by claiming her like my twin suggested, my obsession would plateau. Instead, it's grown to something monstrous and out of my control. I gripped her leash shorter, pulling her close to my side.

"Don't look at anyone. For fuck's sake, don't talk to anyone. Only do what we tell you." *What I tell you.* But I couldn't ask her that with Kash present, and so I didn't.

"What you say," she repeated softly.

"Perfect," I grated out as we reached the Kingman frat house at one end of campus. I didn't bother with the front door where everyone congregated, catching friends and enemies alike. Tonight I used the backdoor, sliding in behind the garden. Kash locked up behind us, pocketing the spare key so no one could follow our path.

"Good girl," he praised Helia as she slipped between dancers without touching anyone, his voice just loud enough to reach me. "Now follow Key, and when he reaches Beau, you do exactly what he says. Do you understand?"

She didn't answer. I twisted back and found her pressed to him, their mouths moving slow and sensuously together. But that wasn't on the cards for tonight. I tugged her leash sharply. She disengaged from my twin with a gasp, trotting to me, her hands pressed to her sides. An apology flared in her eyes, but she didn't mouth it.

Good, because I probably would have spat between those pretty lips before I made her swallow it right here. The urge to shove her to use knees and used her in someone else's house is strong, but not as strong as the need to go home and take my desire out on her until she screamed into my hand for me.

Hell, I would have loved to muffle her prettiest sounds with my fingers crammed into her mouth.

We made it to the living areas where the dancers thinned out. I searched for Bennet, but the head frat boy was conspicuous in his absence. Usually he floated about his own parties, but apparently he was off doing other things tonight. His girlfriend, Silvie, was also not in attendance, and I didn't have to stretch my imagination too far to work out what they were doing for the evening together.

Beau Bennett had plenty of kinks to choose from. In his local community his girlfriend was known by that three letter word that wasn't an acronym, for anything: Toy.

"He's not home." Crush, the captain of the Rippton Allstars ice hockey team, rose from one of the chairs. His girlfriend, Waverly, slid into the space and tugged a pillow in front of her like it might save her from us.

"Do you need help?" She mouthed to Helia.

Cute. I smirked and turned my attention back to Crush. "That's great. Tell him to call me when he's back."

"I'm not his fucking PA. You can run your own comms."

I let him take one step away. "You still owe me a

deal, Napoleon." The extra sports names shit me. They always had.

Crush rolled his shoulders, his shirt stretching hard across the muscle layered beneath. "I remember that scorecard being even. But if you recall otherwise then I'll pay up," he replied evenly, holding my gaze.

Damn, the kid had balls. No wonder he made captain early. It'd be a sorry sight to see him go at the end of the year. As much as I disliked the Kingman frat house in general, we'd lose a solid run of boys at the end of this year.

"I'll see what I can come up with." I wouldn't call him out on it unless I needed him. But it was fun to see him squirm. I did have my asshole factor on tonight, more than usual. I tugged on Helia's collar with her leash. "Time to go."

"We just got here." Surprise blew her eyes wide, though Kash looked as ready to leave as I did.

I wound her in, heedless of our audience until she stood within an inch of me, and leaned down. "We're leaving, wraith. Tonight is done. Is that understood?"

Dark eyes blazed at me, and for the first time, I knew I had a fight on my hands but fuck it, that could wait until we were back at our place, or hers, and then we could deal that shit out in bed together.

"Let us take you home, Little Alice," Kash came in with a different approach. She softened, though her gaze still fixed in mine, blazing and hard. "Let us lead you home and strip you down. Fight us in bed. Fight us when we fuck you., Maybe we could let you run and we could chase you?"

Her lips parted on a soft breath and my blood surged. Fuck, yes I wanted to hunt her down. Let her run and hide in the woods behind the clocktower and find her in the dark.

I waited. "Helia?"

"Alright," she whispered, as though the entire room wasn't hanging on her reply, as well as we were. "I'll come with you."

I nodded curtly, unable to do much more, and strode out the front of the Kingman house less than five minutes after we walked in the back door of the ostentatious building. Kash walked beside me, Helia trotting to catch up. More than once her breath hitched, and I knew that the heels she wore offered torture more than help. Finally, I paused once we were well away from the frat house, but a fair distance from most other places, including the clock tower or the exit to campus that led to the street.

Then I turned on her. "Take the shoes off." I held out my hand for her small bag that I'd let her have for the evening.

Helia paused then tentatively handed it over knowing, I suspected, that she wouldn't get out of this without a fight that she no longer seemed to want.

But I did.

Beside me, Kash shifted on his feet, a sure sign that he'd join me in a moment. "Dress," he murmured.

"What?" Helia backed up a step, forgetting I held her leash. "No. *No.*"

I snapped the leash, pulling her into me. "Dress, Helia. Why don't you fight us more?"

She stared up at me, frowning. "Is that what you want? A girl who runs and screams?"

I stared down at her. "Better than a girl who agrees with everything that I say because someone told you to do it." I wasn't sure until a second before but now I am. Damnit, she was so perfect. So motherfucking perfect. I was sure we found her on our own. Right up until a moment ago, I was sure of it. And now..."

"What?" Helia backed off a step, shaking her head as she glanced between Kash and me. "No. No,

I'm here because–" Confusion brushed across her face. It was almost comical to watch as she came to the same conclusion as I had.

"I think someone swindled us both, Helia. Come on. It's time for some punishment," I said kindly, holding out my hand.

She placed her hand in mine, and my cold fingers folded over her warm ones. Her skin was soft in my grip as she registered my words, and then she pulled back. But it was too late.

"What? Hell, no," she shrieked. "You fucker—"

I unclipped the leather leash and handed it off to Kash. He doubled it over, and slipped it between her lips, effectively silencing her as he stood behind her.

I smiled down at her as she cried and shook for me. And it was the prettiest sight. A sigh left me. "You see, Little Lost Alice, my obsession isn't done yet. I think it's just getting started. So while I know this isn't good for either of us, I can't let you go. But I can make it so you want to run and run and run.... even when you can't." I paused as Kash cut her dress off her with one hand. "Did you tell that girl in the frat house that you were safe? Waverly, was it?"

"Wheeeeee." Her muffled protest were the cutest sound I'd ever heard.

"Wrenlee," Kash interpreted for me.

"Ah, I got it wrong before. Thank you for correcting me." I leaned in and licked her lips around the leather as she began to cry then slid my hand between her legs. She was fucking soaked. I fingered her lightly as she writhed for me. Kash laughed licking and sucking at her shoulders as he ground into her from behind.

"We both want you so bad, Helia," he murmured. "If you survive tonight, maybe we'll take you home and fill all your holes, then leave you out for the drink frat boy to play with."

She shook her head, wild eyes meeting mine laced with fear.

I stroked her face. "I don't know how to forgive, Helia. And I don't know why you've been set in our path. But tonight I'll find out." I kissed her again, mouthing her lips and the leather. "I promise."

"Maaaddddyyy."

Kash looked at me over her shoulder and shrugged. "Who fucking knows."

"Did you bring lipstick, little Alice?" I pawed through her bag and tossed the contents on the grass. Helia sobbed softly. I found a red tube and wrote across her belly as Kash used her collar to wrap her wrists together. I had a spare and backed her up toward a light post. A moment's work and it was done.

"Last touch." I pressed a kiss to her forehead and cut a strip of lace from her dress with my blade. That was tied around her neck as a makeshift collar, the blade dangling low at her belly. "Now, if you don't move, then you don't get cut. If no one touches you..."

I laughed softly.

"Good night, Helia."

CHAPTER ELEVEN

HELIA

They didn't trust me, and I knew why.

But before I could explain any of that to the two men I was fast falling in love with, in our own strange way, I had to endure the bright lights and drunken murmurings of frat boys and sorority girls who took their pictures and couldn't help me because of what Key wrote across my body in my own lipstick.

A shade I'd never be able to wear ever again.

I closed my eyes and dozed between visits. When the next set of footfalls neared, I could barely pry my eyes open. Tonight, of all nights, insomnia failed me. It would only be for yet another camera flash that would be shared across campus come tomorrow anyway. I'd be expelled regardless of how much I could pay out of my personal bank account that I suspected rivaled the twins–together—not that my father cared, since it appeared that he was responsible for putting me in this position.

I'm sending someone to you. Do everything they say.

That plural should have been the first clue. But then I'd seen what the twins were capable of, and m my father's not so veiled threat was forgotten. Even then. It was so obscure that I would never have been able to put it all together.

Nor did I understand his motives. I suspected that part was something between the twins and him, but they'd have to figure it all out themselves. I was done.

Done with dating. Done with men. Give me taco Tuesday and art night and leave me the fuck alone.

"And get me off this stupid fucking lamp post."

"And no more pictures!"

I panted a little after that last one. My throat hurt, too.

"Oh, bravo."

I cracked an eye open to clapping. And found Beau freaking Bennet, the head of the Kingsman frat, standing in front of me. "Go away," I told him tiredly.

"You don't want an audience?" He didn't crack a smile. "Your note suggests otherwise."

I glared at him as he lit his flashlight app on his phone. "Keep it off my eyes please," I said pointedly.

"Oh, you're not the only one who gets light induced migraines. They're horrible things," he agreed, lowering the light to scan my naked body. Light lanced up from the blade anyway as it swung. I squeezed my eyes shut to avoid the glare. "*Touch her and die*," Beau read. "That's not very helpful, is it?"

"Not brilliantly." I had managed to spit out the leash an hour or so back—it felt like an hour ago, and the clock tower chimed at least once since then. I figured it was close to two in the morning, the twins' favorite time.

"So, how do we get you down without touching you?" Beau ran a hand over his chin.

I stared at him. "You can't be serious." I laid it out for him. "They. Will. Kill. You. I've seen them do it," I said earnestly in case he wasn't getting the point. "And not by accident."

"Oh, no," he agreed. "Their murders are completely logical, to them at least. You're their newest obsession. And I don't think you're going away."

"I might be," I grumped. "I'm sick of being treated like this." I leaned forward, tugging at the collar tying my wrists to the light post and winced as the blade cut at my belly with my movements, willing myself still again.

Beau's eyes widened as hot fluid slicked my belly. "Don't do that, Helia. Stay still." He inched forward, studying the set up. "No, I don't think you get a choice. I didn't."

I stared at him and ignored the ache where the blade made a thin cut on my betty like a pendulum swinging. "You were the object of the twins' obsession?"

He cracked a smile, finally. "Not quite. I was their target a few years ago. When I first arrived at Rippton. Ah, here we go." He gripped the handle of the knife and began to cut through my bonds without touching me at all. "Back then, I was the first year student they hated. They set up an elaborate deal and I agreed. Naturally, I didn't get all the information. But they decided enough was enough. So did I. It was a mistake. I had seen enough bad deals to understand this was my last and I accepted the terms." The blade sliced through the leather collar, and I was free.

I rubbed my wrists. "Thank you. What happened?"

Beau shrugged. "They'd never seen anyone accept death before. Everyone fought, they said. No one had grace. And so, they kept me."

A snort bubbled from me. "Like a pet."

His head went to one side. "Like a pet. For a year, maybe. Yes."

Silence fell between us.

"Then what?" I ventured.

Beau offered me a faint smile. "They taught me blades, though I knew some knife fighting. They enhanced my negotiating skills, and I taught them new ways to kill. And they taught me kink. I appreciated it all. Those skills brought me to where I am now."

"Oh." I mulled that over, and collected my ruined dress. "Thank you. I needed to find them and sort this out." I waved vaguely in the direction of the clock tower.

"I'll walk you back," he offered. "Seeing as you might run into trouble who aren't sure what they're getting themselves into."

I cast a look askance at him. "Are you offering to be my guard?"

Beau shook his head. "Nothing so honorable. I hate having to clean up blood before training in the morning."

I huffed back a twisted laugh, and accepted an equally twisted offer.

CHAPTER TWELVE

KEY

Dead Art Buddy Ethan expected us because he'd been told to expect us. Also, Helia's fucking little art friend was high the night we killed him. Which took away from the experience, really, and not at all in a good way.

Kash sat next to me across a desk from Helia's father. To anyone else it might look as though we were simply having a conversation with the sire of the woman we were dating. In a way, we were. This man had been watching us for much longer than we'd seen him. An oversight, from our side. The only difference in this scenario to the former were the guns pressed to the backs of our heads.

I understood why Helia's art buddy behaved the

way he did. I even understood more about Helia, and that I'd been wrong to treat her so harshly. My own fault; I'd seen a stalker where there both was one and also no threat at all. Helia did love us and was ours. If we had a Helia to return to. If our lives were our own after this night.

While I might not be able to forgive another man, I hoped that she would be able to forgive me for how I had treated her. For how we both had.

"Do you understand that the Laurent family fortune was simply never meant to go to a pair of what were then pimply teens?" The man before us laughed. A horrible laugh that I wanted to locate and stuff down his throat until he choked on his own organs and made new sounds. Pleasing ones as breath left his body.

I smiled and leaned forward. "Do you understand that your daughter has the genes of a natural killer?"

That earned me a solid thud across the back of my head with the handgun that had dug a hole into the back of my skull for the past twenty minutes. I shook my head as my vision blurred and spat blood onto the desk before me.

"Don't talk ill of those not here right now," Helia's father spat at me. "She doesn't want to be with either of you. It was my idea to set her in your path. My idea to ensure that you wanted her. My idea—"

"She's been ours for much longer than you've been playing games, old man." Kash ducked the first swipe with the gun but collected the second across the top of his head. He slumped forward with a groan.

"Fuck you, asshole." I launched forward, intent on ending the man's life before mine was snuffed out.

An alarmed noise came from his mouth but the order never arrived.

"Down, boys." A new, smooth voice echoed across the office area inside the warehouse. "Leave us for a few, would you? Do feel free to come back and check on him." Helia strode into her father's office holding a blade.

The blade that was strapped to her throat last night.

"How did you get free?" *Who do I need to kill?*

Her eyes met mine. "Mr Bennett helped me out. He was most useful in cutting me free without touching my skin, or my body in any way." Her lips curled upward. "He's outside now, securing the ground area."

She could call it the perimeter but we'd work on that later.

"Good girl," I murmured. "I'm proud of you."

"Thank you, Key," she murmured and I swore she *glowed*.

"What are you doing here? You should be at Rippton," her father blustered.

"Where you pay me to go so I don't have to think or look at the family business too hard?" Helia lifted a hand that held a pistol of her own and eyed her father with blatant disregard, then us. "Are you being serious? I stop watching for a few minutes and everything goes to hell. Why kill my friends?"

"He wasn't your friend." Kash levered himself up. "Your art buddy was a plant from your father. Paid to follow you around. I think he wanted you to date him. Paid him in tech and cash. I have trails. I never could understand his why. Or his choice to stay here if he was making that much. When I broke into his room he didn't object. I tortured him and he barely moved. Never screamed. Said he expected two of us. We were *expected*. He knew there would be two of us coming for him, Helia."

She nodded her acceptance. "Okay, so what do we do? What now? We know that he sent someone to die. You two kill people all the time. Should I care?"

I watched her, smiling. "Perhaps not. Are we forgiven?"

She tipped her head back. "Are you forgiving of me?"

I never forgive. But you're different. My heart propounded in my chest. "I might be able to work on that."

Her knuckles pressed to my chest was the perfect answer. "Alright. Let's go—"

Her father blustered from behind his desk, unmoving. "The job isn't done, Celia. I told you I had work for you. I want them both dead."

Helia hiccuped a laugh. "I think that's a stupid out loud thought with them in the room," she said gently. "Who is going first?"

She looked between us. Kash patted her.

"This one is your problem, wraith."

"Oh. Threat to those I love, right?" She shrugged, checked the weapon and aimed. "Okay."

The pistol fired, and so did his, raised from under the desk.

Her cry filled the office, but it was his gun that clattered to the ground.

Footsteps clattered up the staircase to the office,

but they were all too late. Their employer had a new face by the time the old mongrel stopped breathing, and Helia's wound was treated.

Beau took her in an ambulance to the local hospital while we managed what we did best.

Clean up.

EPILOGUE

KEY

Leather had always been my favorite scent, apart from Helia's. The two, mixed together?

Motherfucking delicious.

I paused at the steps to the Kingsman frat house to inhale a sensual line along Helia's neck. Her scars she earned the night were on full display, the dress she wore a simple leather sheath held up with an elegant collar and two bands, with cut outs that stopped just above her breast. Those and the rest of her was covered to mid thigh, though her garters and knee high boots told us and everyone else what sort of night this was.

If her dress didn't, Kash and my matching collars and leashes did, along with our assless chaps and reddened bottoms.

She looked like a goddess, and we her servants. As we should be after what she did for us. My cock strained against my pants but I knew we wouldn't be allowed to get off tonight. Not that I minded a little game of denial or two. We would have our fun soon enough. Helia, however, had no such restrictions, and I had no reservations of making her orgasm long and hard on every Kingsman surface I could find.

Tonight was about submission, exhibitionism and worship.... if not necessarily in that order. Because Helia had plenty of fun with us before she left her apartment tonight.

We decided—together—to keep both. Her home, and ours. She loved to paint there, and no one should ruin our girl's peace. That wasn't permissible. And after all she had survived... Helia deserved everything. Including the gift we gave her tonight, in front of everyone.

"What the fuck?" One of the drunken Allstar boys stumbled backwards into his friend. An elbow planted into ribs I wanted to bury my blade between, and imagined twisting. Slowly. Painfully. "Whoa, check out those buns!"

Ignoring the imbecile remarks on the state of my

reddened behind, I held out a hand, Kash mimicking my movements on my other side.

Helia smiled and took the step above us, staring over our heads at the offending frat boys. "You may look and jeer, but don't touch," she said, sweetly. "That pleasure is mine, alone. Come along." She tugged at our leashes, and we followed her, step by step as she paraded us into the house and through to the living areas where their typical, Saturday night post-game party raged.

"So beautiful," Kash breathed, breaking her rule of silence, at the risk of her paddle later, or humiliation now. His fingers flickered at the hem of her leather dress.

She swatted his hands away playfully as I cast him a hard look. "Later," I murmured. "We can wait, brother."

Helia glanced over her shoulder at me, amused by our infighting, apparently. If that's what it took, then that's what we would give her for a good night. She had earned it, after all. But I had at least one more deal to make with our girl, one she would enjoy, even if she didn't understand the terms she agreed to, at first.

But then, they never did. That was the beauty of the deals we made.

Our victims who thought they understood every word but who rarely asked the right questions. Simple, deceitful and oh so fucking pleasurable when they realized how badly they chose afterward when their world came crashing down.

And what she would owe me later.

"Yes, Mistress," Kash said meekly, the fucking liar.

That earned him a pretty little giggle. Helia towed us to the leather recliners that would surely need a wash after this, and planted her ass. One leg crossed over the other as she held our leashes, our naked butts presented to the room.

The silent room that was full of Kingsmen and Allstars who were making out and playing beer pong a moment before. Even the music stopped. Thankfully, because the assholes had terrible taste.

"Jesus Christ, Helia. The fuck did you do to them?" Beau Bennett circled her chair at a safe distance, though his fingers trailed the back.

My eyes met his, my message clear.

His smile in return was soft, and deadly. "Touch her and...yes, I remember. I also remember that she saved *you*. Both of you. Do you remember that?"

I glanced away at the man I had called enemy more than once and might have considered a friend if I didn't want to kill him right now. Instead, I focused on Helia, and my cock swelled in my pants. "I remember."

Her smile was worth everything we did tonight. Everything we have done together. The cost.

Beau planted his elbows on the wings at the back of her chair and leaned over her space. If I didn't have her collar wrapped around my throat, and her leash attached to her hand, I'd rip his intestines out with my bare hand right now. But my little wraith fucking leaned back into his space and gazed up at me, then at Kash. Her tongue licked at her lips, and then her legs opened.

So everyone in the room can see her glistening cunt.

I swear my heart stopped beating. My twin panted for her beside me. My cock raged in pure need.

"Please," I murmured, not caring who hears. Not caring if he heard.

"Louder," Beau said, calm as he slid his fingers through Helia's hair and tugged.

She sighed.

"Kneel."

I didn't know who gave the order, nor did I care. I knelt along with my brother, waiting between her legs where they spread wide for us. The urge to kill Beau dissipated as I waited for her next order, knowing this was a show she put on for us. A torment that she designed for a purpose.

There will be a penance, little wraith of mine.

And we would both enjoy it...maybe even her.

A heel landed on my shoulder, the stiletto point digging in. "Lick."

The scent of her filled my nostrils. I closed my eyes and leaned forward only to be stopped short by her derisive laugh. Beside me, Kash froze, presumably doing the same thing.

"Mistress?" I murmured, risking her displeasure.

"Did you think she'd let you near her yet? You have to earn it, slut." Beau glided his hands along her arms, daring to touch her. His gaze glittered into mine as a third soul joined us.

A tiny form, half my height, or less.

Silvie knelt beside me, shivering in the tiny dress that Beau dressed her in tonight. His Toy. A ridiculous notion—perhaps, if I wasn't the one with my ass on show to the entire fraternity and their sidepieces while I salivated over what I couldn't have.

"Show them, sweet." Helia stroked Silvie's lips with her thumb, barely moving as Beau continued his massage of her arms, apparently with her permission.

And so, I allowed it.

Maybe I could kill him tomorrow. Maybe I wouldn't.

Silvie sighed, settling into her submissive head-space. Her eyes slipped shut as she leaned forward—not to lick Helia's slicked labia, as I had aimed to do, but across my body and lapped at her leather boot.

"Perfect." Helia settled back, snuggling Beau's arms.

A deep growl emanated from my throat, echoed instinctively at my side, the sounds so closely timed that they sounded as one, though I knew she would have caught the fraction of a second's lag.

Helia shot us a hard look that promised more pain and denial, but I didn't care. "We are guests," she murmured. "Have some manners, boys."

I raised my chin and stared her straight in the eye. "My mistress should only be taken care of by the best," I said bluntly. "And he is..."

"Not," Kash said, leaning in to lick at the other side of Helia's boot.

Beau never moved. Helia didn't waver in her resolve.

I shrugged and leaned in to join them, making

sure that as I cleaned the boot with its spiked heel that dug into my shoulder, I chased Silvie's path, a little faster than the sub lost in her dreamy headspace.

When my tongue touched hers and an oath broke above me, I knew I'd won, well before the hand fisted my hair.

Fuck, I didn't care if the fist ended in my face. He was off my girl.

"She tastes sweet." I smiled at Beau's rage filled face, reminding him at a glance that he was the one who put us both in this position to begin with.

He leaned into my face, his shaking hand gripping my white hair so tight I thought he might depart roots from scalp. A fitting end, to wash my sins away in my own blood in this room where I had been so many times when the occupants were passed out or sleeping, whether the head of the house who loomed over me now knew it or not.

"You will not touch her," he hissed in my face. Spittle slammed my skin in tiny, warm pin pricks. "You are not worthy to taste her."

My smile remained as I stared back into his dark eyes, and made my promise. "And you will not die."

Beau's grip tightened in my pale hair, as though he might consider taking it further. A single breath passed between us, where Kash shifted at my side, and Helia's boot dug into my shoulder. I'd bear the mark of her displeasure for a few days, and it would be worth it, but I rejected the string of the blade that Kash pushed into my palm.

I'd hold to my promise, for now. If Beau continued to push me, I'd string him up to the light post where we once tortured our girl and left her on display, the same place he found her and cut her down so delicately in accordance with our rules.

But no one would be able to cut him down after I was done with him.

"Precision. Perfection. Those are our rules." Kash squeezed my fingers, opening my flesh on the blade. His own blood dripped across my palm as he raised the blade.

Beau swore, jerking Silvie away. She huddled in his embrace as Helia had a moment before, only our girl didn't shy away from our blade. It was almost as if she knew and understood what was coming.

Kash licked the blade, mingled with our blood, and leaned the flat against her thigh. She parted her legs wider for him. And offering, maybe. Fuck, my cock strained hard against the leather. I ached for her hands on me, but later. Much, much later.

He rubbed the tip in a circle, making her flesh

redder with each rotation from both the sharpened tip and our fluids.

"How many?" she whispered, staring at him.

He smiled, and rose to crouch over her, whispering in her ear. Her eyes opened wide, her lips parting as he fed her reddened fingers that she sucked on, whimpering and writhing.

Hell, that was a number even I didn't know. I'd never asked, and neither had he. Would she ask me how many I had killed? Would I earn the same reaction from her? Swiftly I began a tally in my head, but it didn't matter—her fingers tangled in his collar as she dragged his mouth to hers. Their kiss was obscene. Sloppy, saliva and blood and tongues.

My neck snapped forward as my leash tugged sharply. I lurched over her thighs, planting my hands at her hips in time to prevent myself from biting my own tongue off. "Close call, wraith," I muttered.

A giggle escaped her as she wriggled her hips upward, dripping her boot from my shoulder. I got the point, or rather, I lost the one digging into my flesh and found hers to tease with my tongue.

A hand caressed my ass from behind as I licked my woman to orgasm while she made out with my twin above me. Fingers traced over my balls and cock through my leathers, working me softly. The sort of softness that teases and shouldn't do anything, but I was so on edge that the lightest touch would make me—

Fuck," I murmured into her pussy as I blew my load, hands free in my pants. Warm cum soaked my leathers and trickled down my thighs as I disgraced myself before her.

"Good little puppy. Lick her clean," Beau's smooth voice mocked in my ear. "Next time she wants to play, I'll let you hump my leg for her pleasure."

For a Kingman, he was a kinky fucker. I should know; I trained him. Still, I groaned, knowing I'd do it. Anything for her, even if I hated him. Maybe keeping him around would be fun after all.

Helia must have heard us as she came against my tongue with a soft cry my twin muffled with his tongue in her mouth. His hand landed on the back of my head, forcing me between her thighs.

I suffocated in her cream, lapping at her until she sighed and he released me.

"Better?" Helia petted me sweetly. Her eyes glowed in the after pleasure of her orgasm, but the power she wielded was more than that.

I nuzzled closer on my leash, letting her delicious scent overwhelm my senses. I'd offer her many more deals in my life, but the one on my tongue right now was the most important.

"I'll worship you forever, my pretty little one. In front of all of them, I'll kneel for you," I breathed. "I'll bow for you." *And only you.*

The gasp around the room was audible, but I didn't give a fuck about any of them. Only for my brother with his lips pressed to her bare thigh as he repeated my words in his own way, making his own deal for her benevolence.

Helia's smile was beatific as she agreed, her eyes glazed with love and desire and obsession. Perfect, for us. And she agreed without another word, just like I expected. Because as always I kept something back. Something just for me.

And my terms were steep.

THANK YOU FOR READING

Thank you so much for reading Helia, Key & Kash's story in ANGEL SHOT. Please leave a review. If you love their serial killer vibe, TWISTED OBSESSION features another artist and a hired hitman in a dark romance set in the same world. READ HERE.
Read other books in Rippton U:

Off Boarding
Vicious Slash
Zero Pointer
Off Stage Fling

Crushing It
Glacial Force

READ ON

Read on for a sneaky chapter of CRUSHING IT

SNEAKY PEEK - CRUSHING IT

NAPOLEON

Highway noise didn't usually bother me, but then, I never experienced it from the inside of a trunk. Road noise roared in my ears. My head swam as I inhaled more carbon monoxide than a body could cope with, and I swore I experienced roadkill every time it splattered on the tires.

The car bumped along beneath my cheek, jolting and jarring me in every direction. Man would the bruises form a pretty pattern come tomorrow. If I was there to see it. Exhaust became my constant companion. Whoever decided to bind me with duct tape had also been sweet enough to leave the trunk ajar. For breathing purposes? I wanted to take hope, but the distinct lack of movement and constant headache left me with one option:

Kill those motherfuckers the moment I got free.

Assuming I got free.

Who the fuck kidnaps the captain of a varsity ice hockey team? Though the answer to that was twofold: today's game, and my father's occasionally questionable business deals.

Light streamed through the small gap wedged open with something that poked me in the cheek. I sucked in enough air to clear my head, discarding that previous thought, and settled on the first option, mainly because it didn't end with me dismembered and in a body bag.

Someone wanted to claim the dubious honor of kidnapping Napoleon 'Crush' Lancaster on game day.

I woke up stuffed into the small compartment and pondered that thought too many times over the last few hours, though it could have been minutes—my sense of time was all screwed up. That they-whoever the hell they were–considered my need to breathe oxygen, albeit air laced with toxic exhaust fumes, gave me hope that I wouldn't be dumped off the edge of a cliff somewhere.

It took more than one man to lift the center and

captain of the Rippton Hails Ice Hockey team as a dead weight.

Not because I'd been drunk at the time; hell, I had a game to play, but because the sick fuckers knocked me out to carry out their little trick.

Reason the nth why my head ached like a mother.

Shafts of light slipped through the tiny gap I sealed my mouth around to claim free air. The sun had risen, slanting light through the breach, and I was in a world of hurt for more than one reason.

We were early in the season, and I needed to get my ass back to Rippton U before I got kicked off the team, taking my dreams of a professional career with it. Like every student at Rippton U, I had enough money in my personal bank account that a hockey career wasn't about the dollar signs or the need to see my face on a commercial selling overpriced water to kids with too much disposable income.

No, my love for the game was my passion. Had been my passion since I was six years old and got slapped in the face with a puck that sailed through the air and brought me my first tooth. But I scored my first goal that day too while I bled like an extra on a slasher flick and fucking loved it.

I thrashed about in the small space and managed

to tenderize myself further and started to take stock for the first time, the tender spots outnumbering my ability to think clearly beyond the throbbing that pounded a staccato beat between my ears. I gritted my teeth and pushed up on my duct taped hands. Arching my back I shoved them against the roof of my cage, yelling my frustration when it didn't budge.

Enough was enough, and I gave myself permission to lose my shit when some asshole kidnapped me and stuffed me in a small space.

It was a damn good thing that I had no claustrophobic tendencies. I just wouldn't have a career if I didn't get my ass back to Rippton soon.

I wouldn't have a career.

Fuck me.

"You assholes stop the car! I'll rip you a new one if we don't stop this fucking charade now!" My voice cracked at the end of my roar, ending on a cough that consumed me. I'd do more than rip whoever I had to a new one when I got free. It made me feel better not to be a passive participant in my own abduction, though.

To my total and utter surprise, the car slowed. I slid to the back of the trunk then the other direction, my head thumping against the small wall that separated the hatch of the car and the back seat, and back toward the car's exterior.

And we stopped.

Every inch of me needed to rant, to throw myself at the trunk lid, but I saved that unfurling energy for the fight coming my way. Flexing my fingers and toes, I urged as much circulation into my limbs as I possibly could. Pins and needles stung me, but I'd experienced worse pain, and besides, I could use it.

The lid of the trunk popped open. Light streamed in, obliterating my vision worse than the arena lights on game night. I blinked watering eyes that I couldn't shield.

Hands grabbed at me. I thrashed frantically, one sense already useless. With my hands and feet restricted by the duct tape, I had little hope of actually doing significant damage.

What I wouldn't give for a hockey stick and the freedom to swing it right now.

Disembodied hands hauled me out of the car and before my eyes could adjust to the indescribably cheery brightness that flared my vision out, some bastard punched me in the face.

I hit the dirt beneath my bare feet, grit scraping my cheek.

Well, that wasn't very nice at all. I had never fully appreciated the flat surface of a highway until now.

I pushed up from the ground, blinking at grit that blurred before me as a puff of hot exhaust hit my cheek at far too close quarters. Gravel showered me as the car pulled away. I raised my bound hands over my face in a belated effort to protect myself and sucked in a breath filled with carbon monoxide.

Adding hacking my lungs out on the side of the highway to my list of injuries, I sat absolutely still, taking in my surroundings.

Desert spread to one side of me, a constant stream of cars flowing in the other direction. I patted my jean pockets awkwardly with both hands but came up empty. Had I been dumped in the middle of Death Valley? My stomach turned over at the thought. That was more than a three hour drive back to the game. But the highway had too much traffic to be completely out in the desert. I hoped.

No phone, and no fucking idea where I had been dumped. I hadn't even had enough sense to memorize the license plate before my assailants drove away.

A few horns honked, but their drivers didn't slow. I offered them a one-fingered salute behind my back as I worked at the tape wrapped around my ankles, but with bound fingers, all I achieved was to add more bruises to my plight as I brought myself to my knees.

No signs lined the blacktop to tell me *which* damn highway I knelt on the side of like a Sunday hooker on a Monday morning. The beeping around me increased. I ignored them, sawing uselessly at my wrists. Before I could free myself, an old hatchback pulled up beside me.

Desiccated roadkill and smog assailed me a second time as the car over shot my position.

It came to a stop eventually and reversed with caution. The car pulled up, pointed in the opposite direction to the cars passing me on my side of the highway. The driver must have crossed four lanes of highway traffic to pull across to me.

Did that make the newcomer my friend or my enemy? I clenched my teeth and tried to push up to my feet, but I only succeeded in making a greater ass of myself as I toppled sideways.

The door opened as I righted myself. I clenched my teeth, expected the worst, and waited. What other fuckery headed my way this morning?

A pair of slim, toned legs encased in smooth black pants swung out from the driver's seat. I blinked. They looked sprayed on from the ankles up.

My cock decided now was a good time to function, having not gotten its morning wood out of the way, and reminded me sharply of my desperate urge to pee that I had blessedly forgotten in my rush from my dorm to my current situation.

The fuckers stole me direct from my dorm.

Nothing like being knocked out and stuffed in the back of a car after a pre-dawn run, especially when they had been considerate enough to let me down over a gallon of water in the aftermath of my light workout on game day before kidnapping me.

The need to relieve myself warred with my desire to inflict serious damage on the assholes who had manhandled me, but when the driver stepped out of the car, I forgot everything, even my name.

Until she said it.

"Napoleon Lancaster? The Emperor?"

Hearing my nickname got my attention. I squinted in the brightness, still headachy and adjusting after so long in a cramped space, but I didn't recognize her.

Dressed in those spray on plastic or leather looking pants, black high heels topped with a blue sweatshirt that gave her a sexy-comfy vibe I instantly liked. Her straightened blonde hair shimmered down her back. She looked like she'd stepped right out of a damn magazine.

As captain of the college ice hockey team I had my fair share of puck bunnies, but this girl blew them all away.

"Yeah?" I managed to croak while my eyeballs bugged from my head.

She stopped a few feet from me, her hands planted on those gorgeous fucking hips with curves that went for miles, her heels shoulder width apart.

I knelt at her feet and worshipped her.

A faint smile played on lush soft pink lips. "Would you like some help? Frat prank gone wrong? I thought you'd be the one pulling a stunt like that."

"I wish," I grunted. "And thanks for the vote of confidence. Wait, where do you know me from?"

The smile brightened. "Rippton U. Couldn't leave one of our precious athletes in distress." She turned to display an Ice Phoenix printed across the back of her sweatshirt. The team slogan, *Reborn, Rise, Conquer* slashed across its extended wings in bold print. The entire image was wreathed in icy blue flame. She looked at me over her shoulder, and I realized her ice blue gaze matched the phoenix.

"That's stunning." Was I talking about her or the sweatshirt? "I don't remember anything that amazing coming from merchandising." I should know, I had a closet full of the stuff that got sent out to us whenever they added new items to the list. Which seemed to be every second month.

"Thanks. My roommate designed it. She's a digital game design major but she does logos and all sorts of amazing stuff."

"She's got talent. What's your name?"

"Wrenlee Cheshire. Like the fucking cat. No jokes," she warned as my eyes lit up.

"Sure, kitten."

The way her mouth popped out in a pink moue, her eyes blazing as they narrowed was worth it, even if she never spoke to me again.

"Fuckboy."

"Probably." I grinned and raised my wrists. "Help a player out?"

Her smile turned wicked as she withdrew a slim blade from her back pocket. "Not a problem."

My mouth went dry. "Ah, that's not what I—" I broke off as she slipped the sharp edge straight through the tape at my wrists and had done my ankles by the time that I picked the tape from my arms. The tattered pieces held far too many of my hairs as their trophies, but I couldn't argue with being free.

Plus, I had a game to play.

"Thank you. Is there a chance of getting back to Rippton in a hurry? I don't even know where we are."

"They did a job on you, didn't they? What did you do? Never mind, don't answer that." She held up a hand to halt a protest that died a short death on my lips. "It's forty minutes back. Hop in." She gestured to her car.

I wouldn't last that long. The memory of the water I'd drunk at the gym tweaked the rising pressure. "Uh..." I received a raised eyebrow for my efforts. "It's been a while," I waved vaguely at the area in front of my crotch. "I need to—" I gave her a pained smile, turning my back to the passing traffic. My options were to either sit in pain for the next near hour or choose a foot high desert bush to pee on.

"Oh!" Her face flaming, she spun around in my peripherals. A moment later the car door slammed behind her.

I hoped she wouldn't drive off on me while I relieved myself.

Read CRUSHING IT

ABOUT THE AUTHOR

USA Today Bestselling author Sofia Aves writes fast-paced police romances, sizzling military units, steamy cowboys with a Montana backdrop and the occasional cheeky god. Sofia writes kidlit for charity and has over one hundred and fifty publications across five not-so-super-secret pen names. She's the acquisitions editor for Evernight and Evernight Teen publishing and is a mum of three crazies in a returned veteran household. Sofia has two overly large fur babies who think they're teacup puppies.

Sofia lives near Brisbane, Australia where she has her own alpaca park, Lorendel.

www.sofiaaves.com

Sign up to Sofia's newsletter and get a free Blue Blooded Brothers book.

Haven't read the Z Boy's prequel? Get it for free here:
A TABLE FOR TEN

READ SOFIA'S SERIES

Blue Blooded Brothers

Collision

Politics & Paperwork

Blindsided

Sentinel

Mugshots & Candy Canes

Impact

Reckoning

Red Hart Ranch

Snow on the Range

Siren on the Range

Sundown on the Range

Spirit on the Range

Ash on the Range

Mistletoe on the Range

Forgotten Mountain Man

Texan Devils

Ranger's Wish

Ranger Bedevilled

Ranger's Passion

Ranger's Fury

Ranger's Wrath

Ranger's Storm

Snapdragons & Seductions

Summer with a Ranger

Merry with a Ranger

Beach Duty Collection

Playing to Win

Off Boarding

Vicious Slash

Zero Pointer

Off Stage Fling

Rippton Allstars

Crushing It

Glacial Force

Rippton Creatives

Study Games

Make Me, Break Me

Twisted Obsession

Spring Break with a Mafia Prince

A Royally Fake French Menage

Angel Shot

Jericho Chimeras

Puck Me Always

Puck My Heart

Puck me Sideways

Z Boys

King

Joker

Hearts

Ace

Mayhem & Mistletoe

Ruski

Fast Track to Love

Speed Trap

Klauss Brothers

Zander

Keegan

Gallo Empire *with Jade Marshall*

Splintered Vows

Fractured Vows

Fierce Vows

Savage Covenant

Rom Coms

She's A Hot Christmas Mess

Boats, Moats and Root Beer Floats

Writing Romantasy as
SOFIA SHELLEY
Dead Poets Sorority

Writing Reverse Harem Dark Romance as
DOVE PRIEST
Recurve Ridge

Kidlit writing as
JO SEYSENER
The OCD Elf
The OCD Elf's Great Reindeer Calamity
Greg and the Egg

writing YA as
JOSS PHOENIX
Alchem Academy
HIDE FROM US

Writing spicy paranormal romance as
RAVEN HUSH
Club Fray
Darkest Desires
Purge
Kidnapped By Claws
Ruin

Shadow Lords

Sinner's End

Heaven's Gate (2026)

Monster Brides

Phoenix's Eternal Flame

Kraken's Vow

Krampus' Christmas Bride

Silent Sentinels Duet

Reflections of Silence

Echoes in the Void

Monsters In New York

Feral Moon Rising